Kragg and Pa fired at each other at the same instant, and it looked like both shots hit their mark as both men staggered backward. Pa's shot had hit Kragg in the arm, spinning him to his left so that he faced us.

And friend, you never seen two brothers do anything so fast, so accurate, and so right at one time. Nathan and I raised our Colts and fired, almost as one shot. Both slugs hit Kragg in the chest, sent him staggering to the rear.

If he wasn't already dead on his feet, when Tom Dobie stepped out from behind those skittish horses at the hitch rail and let fly with his shotgun, he damn sure was. . . .

FAWCETT GOLD MEDAL BOOKS
by Jim Miller:

COMANCHE TRAIL

GONE TO TEXAS

SUNSETS

WAR CLOUDS

Jim Miller

FAWCETT GOLD MEDAL • NEW YORK

A Fawcett Gold Medal Book
Published by Ballantine Books
Copyright © 1984 by James L. Curtis

Library of Congress Catalog Card Number: 84-91065

ISBN 0-449-12483-5

Manufactured in the United States of America

First Ballantine Books Edition: November 1984

To Myrna Porter, for patience and understanding, and for believing me when I told her how hard this job can be at times.

Chapter 1

I saw them before I heard them. It was midday and I was about to get a drink when I saw the tiny puff of smoke on the horizon.

"Visitors." I said it to myself, the way a man does when he has been alone for some time. Or maybe it was because Nate, Ellie and James had always been there to talk to and now were not. They were likely back East somewhere now, visiting with Ma and Pa, who had never seen their first grandson, James. Me, I stayed behind, figuring it would be something special to my brother and his wife to be able to show off their son to our folks. He was a right smart boy, James was, and I reckon I was about as proud of him as Nate and Ellie could be.

Besides, someone had to mind the ranch we had. It was a small one to be sure, but it was a start; and after being here in Texas for some ten years, Nate and I were making a fair go of it. When he agreed to go on the trip, I knew that my brother, restless as he was, was going to enjoy himself just being with Ma and Pa again. But I didn't let him off the hook that easy. Nosiree. I made sure he give me his word that he'd bring me back a goodly share of books to read, and then I made Ellie promise to keep an eye on him to see he got it done. We had all laughed about it then, but I reckon in the back of our minds, all of us knew the real reason for the trip. It was to show off James.

All of this crossed my mind as I automatically reached for my rifle and pistol nearby, my sight never leaving the cloud of dust as it got bigger and the noise of hoof beats became more apparent.

The corral post I was working on could wait.

I leaned the rifle against the front door of the cabin and dipped a gourdful of water from the rain barrel, smiling to myself as the cool liquid dripped down my chest. It wasn't what you'd call a real rain barrel. Actually, it was an oversized whiskey barrel I had brought back from San Antonio de Bexar one time. And Ellie kept reminding me that if the Temperance people ever ventured this far west, they would condemn the Callahans for sure because the water still held a hint of whiskey to its taste.

The riders came into sight then, and I eased the grip on my pistol, tucking the Colt into my waistband. There were a half-dozen of them that I could see, led by what appeared to be a grizzled old man. When he came into clearer focus I took in the features of Ab Sharpson. The man wore a blue work shirt like mine, but that was the only similarity between us. Ab wore a frock coat and dress trousers of an eastern gambler, minus the velvet vest. The coat could never be buttoned for the protruding potbelly in its way, and if he did not look ridiculous enough, the presence of the bowler hat atop his head and the shaggy, frayed hair sprouting from beneath it was the kicker. And somehow I could never remember seeing him without at least a week's growth of beard, something Ellie would never tolerate in Nate or me.

"Need volunteers, Finn," the old man said in a hurry, pulling his horse to a halt and dismounting at the same time. "Raise your right hand," he continued without hesitation. "Do you solemnly swear to uphold the . . . oh, hell, what am I doing?" he asked in disgust. "You're good for it."

"Now, wait a minute, Ab. Why don't you just tell me what I'm supposed to be volunteering for?"

"Comanch'." I handed him the gourd of water and he took a deep pull on it as he caught up his breath. Handing it back to me, he said, "It's Johnston. Old Homer says he spotted a few braves day or two back didn't look too friendly."

"You sure?" I asked, handing the gourd to the others who had dismounted for a drink. "Homer Johnston gets spooked kind of easy, as I recall," I said with a smile. But trying to make light of a bad situation had little effect on Ab.

"I reckon that could be, Finn," he said with a patience that sounded a bit on the thin side. "You could probably say them steers of Homer's died of fright, too, ugly as them Comanch' are." Then the face and voice hardened as one, and he spit the words out as if they were a part of the cud of tobacco he kept in his jowls. "But I'd lay money it was more likely the arrows he found in 'em did it! Now, you coming or not?"

"Lemme get my horse," I said. "Trough's around to the side. You might as well belly-up your mounts while I'm getting ready." In this country you took real good care of your neighbors and trusted them to do the same for you when the occasion arose. It was the way of things.

Homer Johnston lived some ten miles from our spread, but we were too late when we got to his house, knew we were late when we spotted the smoke on the horizon.

"Damn!" Fat as he was, Ab Sharpson was the first to dismount when we reached the charred remains of the house. The stock had been driven off, and it seemed that everything in sight that was burnable had been put to the torch. But it wasn't the scorched timber that Ab was swearing at. He was shaking his head when I dismounted, and when I saw what he was staring at, I felt a twinge in my stomach, the kind that makes you want to be sick. "Long as I been with the Rangers, I never gotten used to it, Finn, never."

"Don't see how a body could."

Homer Johnston lay on the porch, several arrows in his chest, a pool of blood at the base of his skull where the Indians had hatcheted a small piece of scalp for their coup count. At one time or another most of us had seen firsthand or heard from a friend what happened to the victim of a scalping. But the all-too-visible sight within the walls before us was enough to turn a man's stomach. Johnston's wife and eight-year-old daughter lay inside the ruins. No one would ever know whether the two had been tortured or raped before they died, for the bodies were unrecognizable lumps of black. A slight breeze came up, and the horses got wind of the stench, veered away from it.

"We'll come back to bury 'em," Ab said, gathering the reins of his horse. "This trail don't look too promising, but let's see where it leads to."

"You sure you want to do that?" One of the men spoke up in an uncertain voice, for we all knew that Ab Sharpson did not take to being questioned. "Seems to me they's a lot of tracks here. Enough for a good-size war party."

"Garvey"—Ab spit out the man's name—"I'll follow these heathens to the dark side of hell if it'll give me a chance at killing 'em!" His eyes hardened, and the voice took on a tone of righteous indignation as he stared at Garvey, jerked a thumb over his shoulder at the smoldering cabin. "Ain't nobody deserves to die like that. Nobody! So we're going after these murderers until we find 'em or they disappear from the face of this earth. Now, if you don't think you can stomach that line of thought, sonny, you get out of my outfit and out of my sight, understand?"

There was a long silence, and it didn't take much to see that Garvey wanted in the worst way to defy Sharpson, but would not—or couldn't. I had never liked the man, considered him to be one of those who were gutless unless reinforced by numbers.

"What's the matter, Garvey," I said in a none-too-friendly manner, "your stomach getting squeamish?" If there was a bite to the way I said it, well, it was meant that way. Like I said, I wasn't too fond of this fella, and most of those riding that day knew it as well. There was a long silence then while we all of us waited for a reply, but Garvey had none.

Finally, he reined his horse to the right and took off at a lope, following the tracks.

We followed the trail into late afternoon. Whoever they were, these renegades made no pretense of hiding their path, for it was an easy one to follow. But we must have been so caught up in looking at the ground for tracks that it wasn't until near sundown that we realized we had ridden a complete circle. Ab Sharpson must have been the first one to notice it, for I was still concentrating on the tracks when he dropped back to my side.

"Finn," he said and pulled to a halt.

When I looked up, he was pointing to the smoke on the horizon. I followed the glance, squinting at the far-off structure. At first it was simply another homesteader's cabin in flames, much like Homer Johnston's. But looking at it a few seconds longer, I noticed a familiarity to it, and when I turned to Ab I could feel the anger rising to my face.

Without a word, I slapped the reins across my horse's rump as hard as I could, digging my heels into the animal's side as I raced across the plains, the rest of the group not far behind me.

All that ran through my mind then was that they were burning our house! Ain't nobody had a corral as big as ours! And, damn it, I was the one that built it! And right along with it was my concern for Ellie and James, but then I remembered they were back East with Nathan and the fear eased some. Now it was anger I had to deal with, and from what I was seeing as I closed in on the cabin, I could practically guarantee it would be a long time getting rid of it.

Pulling up in front of the cabin, it could have been the Johnston place all over again and what it must have looked like in its last stages of destruction, before the fire died out. The livestock were all gone. The two horses and handful of maverick longhorn steers were nowhere in sight. Even the Conestoga wagon Nathan, Ellie and I had come out here in ten years ago was in flames.

"I'm sorry, Finn," Ab said, pulling up beside me. "I really am."

"Damn it! If I hadn't been with you, this wouldn't have happened!" I said it hard and even to Ab, trying to remain as calm as I could, knowing it was all but impossible.

"I know how you feel, son, but before you go to cussing me any more, you might want to take one other thing into consideration."

"What?" If I sounded defiant, it was because I was feeling that way.

"If me and the boys hadn't volunteered you, you'd be as dead as Homer Johnston right now."

Chapter 2

We never did find the war party that raided our area and burned our ranch down. But I reckon that might not have been too unusual then. It was the spring of 1846 and we had more than Indian troubles to worry about. At least, if any of the rumors that were circulating were anywhere close to true. It had been ten long years since San Jacinto and Texas independence, but it was looking like those same war clouds that had gathered over Texas then were heading our way again.

Annexed and recently accepted into statehood, Texas seemed to be nothing more than a pawn in a game of international affairs in which relations between the governments of the United States and Mexico were left strained, to say the least. Diplomatic talks had broken off and for nearly a year now General Zachary Taylor of the army had been camped on the Nueces River as a precautionary force in case of open hostilities.

Whether the Nueces River or the Rio Grande was the border separating the two countries had always been a disputed question. The Mexicans claimed the Nueces was, the Americans the Rio Grande, even though the 120 miles separating them was a desolate, barren land. Then, not long after the ranch had burned, General Taylor and his forces moved to Point Isabel, at the southernmost part of the Rio Grande. And when word of that came down, it wasn't long before Ab Sharpson and his boys showed up again.

"Hays is looking for volunteers, Finn," Ab said one day after he'd been to headquarters. Ab and his Rangers had spent over a week trying to track down that war party while I did what little I could to salvage the remains of our ranch, corral and livestock. "Seems this Taylor fella might be getting his little army into a fracas and Jack's volunteered to furnish him Rangers for scouts and such. Thought you might be interested."

"I don't know, Ab," I said. Normally, I would have welcomed the chance, if for no other reason than to break the monotony of running a spread. But this was different; this was no ordinary situation. "Nathan's gonna bring back the family soon, and I'm gonna have to find us someplace to call a home."

"Oh, hell, Finn"—Sharpson grinned—"won't be but a week, ten days at the most. You know what kind of army them Mexicans got. Why, shoot, boy, you'll have plenty of time to build you a place. In fact, me and the boys will help you do it! How's that?"

What he was saying made sense. I could remember San Jacinto and Nathan's stories about how the only times the Mexicans had ever won a battle was when they outnumbered their foe, and even then, at San Jacinto, they turned tail and ran. I had taken to studying the culture of the people and really liked it, but when it came to fighting, I had to agree with Nathan. These Mexicans were as inferior as hell!

"When do we leave?"

"Good lad. I knew I could count on you."

We left the next day; the same group of us who a short time ago had been chasing Comanches were now headed for duty as scouts to the United States Army. Yet I got a feeling that day as we rode off. Maybe I was the only one who had it, but it was one of those things in the back of your mind that tell you something just ain't right. And that kind of feeling usually pans out when it has its beginnings in your gut. I could particularly feel it in the presence of Garvey. There was just something about the man that didn't ring true. He was devious, a loner; of that I was sure. Not that being a loner was that uncommon on the frontier, for many men prized their freedom in that way. In fact, if Nathan had not found Ellie, I would have bet he'd've turned out a loner himself. But this man, this Garvey, would sell out to the other side if the price was right. Of that I was also sure.

It was our second night out, when a passerby stopped

for a meal, that I knew we were in for trouble without a doubt. He never did give his name, but then, I didn't care for him much either. A happy-go-lucky sort, he had spent most of the meal bragging about how great he was at playing Seven-up, casually mentioning that he was with a Ranger spy company. The fact that no one knew of him, nor he them, didn't make much difference to the rest; but me, I had thoughts of my own on him. When I came back from checking my horse and gear, he was still there, seeing how much sweat he could work up on his upper lip.

"Lived eight days on one scrawny chicken and a coupl'r berries," he was saying, holding the others' attention. "Ninth day come and we finally struck us some good luck."

"Yeah?" one of the group acknowledged encouragingly.

"Yup. Horse give out. Broke down plumb on the spot in the center of that prairie. And you know, there wasn't a stick big enough to tickle a rattler with, much less kill the poor thing. So I saved him by shooting him. Hell, three more minutes and he would've died nateral anyway. Now, boys, butchering him and putting them chunks of meat on our ramrods was easy enough, but let me tell you, the cooking was another thing again. See, I gathered up all of this prairie grass into a heap big pile and set it to fire and—" At this point, the man stopped and shrugged, a hopeless look on his face.

"Well?"

"Well, it flashed up like powder and went out just as quick."

"But how did you cook your horsemeat?" one of the younger listeners asked.

"Why, the fire caught on to the high prairie grass and the wind kinda carried the flames streaking across the prairie. Well, I did my dangdest to run alongside that fire and hold that chunk of meat near as I could, and I gotta tell you that for a long ways it was nip and chuck. I tell you, you never did see such a race!"

"But did you cook your meat in the end?"

"Not bad, I didn't. Chased that damned fire a mile and a half till it run right into a wet marsh and the fire and horsemeat come out even—a dead heat, especially the meat."

"But was it cooked?"

"Cooked!!" The stranger's face screwed up so all of the wrinkles were visible, forming a look of pure disgust. "Nah! Just crusted some. You see, son, you don't cook broke-down horseflesh that easy anyhow." He paused a moment, rubbing his chin in thought. "One thing I never will be able to decide, I reckon, is what was the tougher, the meat or the job."

There was general laughter in the group, and I found myself momentarily laughing with them.

"Say, where you boys heading, anyway?"

"Down to Taylor's outfit down on the Rio," Ab Sharpson said.

"Oh." There seemed to be a sadness in his voice now, but I thought I saw the man try to cover it with a leer of the eye. "Going down 'mongst the robbers on the Rio Grande, are you? Well, fine times you'll have, boys." The man paused and a serious look came to him now as he continued. "I been there my own self, you know. Done something you fellers won't, though."

"How's that?" I asked.

"I come back." It was nothing more than a statement of fact, but I wasn't the only one who cocked a suspicious eye toward the man and waited for him to speak. "It's pure and nateral hell down there, boys," he finally said in near desperation.

Ab Sharpson, who had been on the outskirts of the group, now crowded his way through, stood before the stranger, hands on hips, a frown forming on his forehead.

"You want to add some to that, friend? I got a feeling this is one story I don't want to miss."

"Well, there's talk, you see?" The man grew suddenly nervous, the look on his face one of pure doubt about whether or not he would get away from camp alive.

"What kind?"

"When I come from back East a ways, they were talking about this new Mexican army having more than twice the troops we do. Then when I got down on the Rio, I got to thinking maybe there was some truth to that." He took a fidgety glance over his shoulder to see how close his horse was. "Look, boys, I've got to get going. I'm obliged for the meal and all, but—"

"I want to hear the rest of that story." Ab placed a firm hand on the man's shoulder, and if he didn't know then and there that he wasn't leaving until Ab got what he wanted, he was flat-out dumb.

"You ask Sam Walker when you get down there, if he's still alive. That man don't worry much about dying."

"Ask what?"

"I was with him when he took his men on a scouting mission a few days back." A look of shame came over him now, and he flushed as he spoke, looking at the ground. "Sixty-some got killed after they was captured. Only a handful of us got out alive. Walker was one of them." Then silently the man rose, walked to his horse and mounted it.

"Let him go," Ab said when I took a step in the man's direction. Then, as the stranger turned to go, he said, "Son?" The rider glanced over his shoulder. "You done fine. Thanks."

That was when I knew for sure there was trouble up ahead. I could feel that twinge in the pit of my stomach as I thought of Sam Walker, a good friend of Nate's and mine. He was one of the best known of the Texas Rangers. Some say second only to Jack Hays himself.

From what this fella had said, it sounded like there was a war on, and maybe we hadn't heard of it yet was all. Watching the stranger ride, I had a feeling Ab Sharpson's prediction of a ten-day skirmish was going to be a little bit off.

Chapter 3

As it turned out, the stranger was far from accurate in the telling of his version of "natural hell" on the Rio Grande. It seems that General Zachary Taylor's army of two thousand had been playing a cat-and-mouse game with the Mexican forces, probing and then eluding the greater forces of General Arista. According to the scouts' estimates, we'd be going up against anywhere between five and fifteen thousand enemy troops, but it sure wasn't the "natural hell" that fella spoke about. Maybe because a lot of the boys down in that area had participated in the Texas Revolution ten years before and started telling stories about the Alamo and Goliad and how the Mexicans butchered the forces there; or maybe it was telling all of these greenhorns that most all of the skirmishes we had fought against the Mexicans had been against bigger forces. Maybe that was what scared them.

But for all of those who might keep such stories in mind when going into battle, there were those you can only describe as nerveless. And that was the perfect description of Sam Walker.

Of slight build, his perpetual slouch and pale blue eyes made him appear harmless enough; however, those associated with him knew of his reputation as a fearless combatant who rarely brought back prisoners, particularly those of Mexican descent. And rightly so, for he was one of the few survivors of the ill-fated Mier Expedition of 1842, and those who made it back were especially hateful toward the Mexican government and resentful about the humiliation and degradation they were subjected to as prisoners before they were finally released.

Most agreed that that experience in itself had made Sam Walker the most effective scout in General Taylor's spy system. But if old Sam had been in any fighting of late, he didn't seem to be any the worse for wear as Ab Sharpson and I found him at Point Isabel, where General Taylor's army was camped.

"That fella's either got the wrong war or the wrong Walker," Sam said after I told him the story we had heard. "Maybe he's thinking of that Thornton fella, who took sixty-some men across toward Matamoras a week or so back. Seems I heard that sixteen of 'em were killed and the rest captured."

"No, he said sixty. I'm certain." Sharpson frowned. "What happened to those men that got taken, anyway?"

Sam shrugged. "Hard telling. Far as we know, they're still alive, but you know how the Mexes can be." There was a note of hatred in his voice as he said it, and no one needed to ask how it came to be there.

"When we come in, I stopped by Jack Hays's outfit, and he said we'd be tagging along with your boys," Ab said.

Sam smiled. "Fine with me, Ab. Have your men find a spot and spread their rolls. Just don't make it permanent. From what I've been hearing, I think Old Rough 'n' Ready Taylor's starting to take this war serious. And I'll tell you, friends, when he gets to moving, there isn't gonna be much he'll stop for."

"Yeah, I've got to give him credit," Ab said. "He ain't no West Pointer, like most of these young bucks, but the man sure can soldier."

Ab left then—to bed down the men, he said—but I figured Ab knew it had been a long time since Sam Walker and I had visited each other, and was likely just getting out of the way. Nathan had been down Mexico way a few years back and Sam had helped him out of a tight spot and the two had become fast friends. That was before the Mier Expedition. Not many who'd returned from that were too keen on talking about it, so we spent a goodly share of time catching up on old times.

"Still wearing the same old thing, I see," Sam said, staring down at the crude holster positioned on my left hip. The leather holster concealed the body of the pistol, leaving only the butt thrusting forward, but it was only the handle that Sam Walker needed to see to identify it. After all, a man should know his own designs, and it was Sam who had suggested the modification of the butt of the Paterson Colt back in 1839.

"Yeah," I said, pulling it out and balancing it in my hand. "I'm surprised it's lasted as long as it has. No, Sam, can't complain."

I remembered hearing Nathan tell of how Walker had suggested to Sam Colt that the grip of the revolver be reshaped to better fit the hand. Along with that change Colt had added the loading lever, directly under the barrel. Sam Colt had been quick to patent the procedure, for it made reloading both quicker and easier, freeing the shooter from having to break the weapon down into three separate sections as had to be done with the original Paterson revolver. Now all that was needed was to properly apportion one's powder and drop in the lead balls before ramming them home with the newly designed lever and capping the cylinders in order to shoot. Henceforth, Colt's repeaters had been immensely popular among the Texas Rangers and were given Sam Walker's own approval when he fought in the Seminole Wars in Florida in 1837 and 1839 under the same Zachary Taylor he was now serving. We called it a "Texas Paterson" or a "Walker Paterson," but whatever its name, this was the type of weapon that was becoming more and more a necessity for survival on the frontier. Most men who owned a Colt wouldn't hesitate to tell you so either.

"You know, Finn, I've been thinking about writing Sam Colt about some more improvements."

"That so?"

"Yes," he said, taking the weapon from my hands. "You see, I was thinking maybe he could fix up something down around the trigger to protect it, sort of like the trigger guards on our rifles.

"And a heavier load. Most of 'em are thirty-six calibers, but even the forty-ones like this need more wallop to them. Hell," he said, shrugging, "for that matter, the whole gun needs to be heavier, leastwise for the kind of fighting we're going to be getting into."

"Sounds good," I said enthusiastically. "Sam took to

your first ideas, so he ought to take to these, too. Besides, it might be just what he needs to get back into business."

Even with the popularity of the Paterson revolver, Sam Colt hadn't been able to get what he so desperately needed to help him sustain his business, a contract to furnish weapons to the United States Army. He had successfully manufactured and sold his "five-shooter" to the Texas Navy as well as the Texas Rangers, and those individuals desiring to purchase the gun. But the Army had tested the weapon and found it to be too fragile to take the punishment a trooper's life would give it. So it seemed logical that Sam Walker's idea of a more solidly built handgun would appeal to Sam Colt, who had gone into bankruptcy in 1842 and had been out of the arms business ever since.

"Things settle down," Sam said, "I'll write a letter to Sam."

It wasn't until the following day that we understood why Taylor's army of two thousand men had traveled only five miles the day before. I recalled that long trek we had made with Sam Houston and his force, almost half the size of Taylor's army, just prior to the Battle of San Jacinto. We had gone much further on far less and in weather that was some of the worst in the history of Texas. So it didn't seem unreasonable to expect a group twice that size to march more than five miles in one day. It was the sight of Taylor's supply train and artillery group that morning that changed our minds.

"Now, would you look at that," Ab said in mild amazement as we looked down on the operation from a grassy knoll a ways from the camp. We had been up, fed and gone before daylight, scouting out the area ahead just to be doing something. It was two hours past sunup when we returned to find Taylor's men strung out in a line of march that covered more than a mile, while the base camp before them still appeared to be a muddle of confusion.

"Ask me," one volunteer said, "that general come to homestead, not fight a war."

"Could be, could be."

The remuda we had spotted riding in the day before was considerable, which was to be expected for a force of two thousand men. But out of the whole two thousand, only 275 were cavalry, and they all belonged to the Ranger forces of Jack Hays and Sam Walker. Most all of Taylor's men were infantry and artillery and traveled afoot. The remuda turned out to be a mixture of horses and mules that were used to transport the two hundred supply wagons and artillery pieces. Looking down on them now from that hill, I could see two teams of twenty oxen each straining as they pulled the clumsy eighteen-pound cannons which were Taylor's largest artillery. Maybe that was normal for an army, but Taylor and his boys wouldn't find many who approved of such things. Like it or not, he was in a land where the light cavalry horsemanship of the Comanche and those of us who'd come to settle in this land was the acknowledged way of combat. Out here you stood your ground and fought your enemy toe-and-heel if you expected to keep what you had, along with a healthy reputation for your ability to fight. Anything else would have been "homesteading," like that one volunteer said.

We passed some of those infantrymen on our way into camp, hearing the usual complaining such men do, but I noticed that they seemed to have an optimistic outlook about them, almost as if their prayers had been answered. When I did some checking around, I found out why. It seems Sam Walker had slipped out of camp the night before and done some more reconnaissance in enemy territory, finding out that a known campsite of the Mexicans was deserted. So word was being spread up and down the line that the Mexican army was retreating and Taylor's men would meet no opposition upon reaching their destination.

Pa always said that a little bit of fear was good, for it gave a man reason to be cautious, whereas too much fear could ruin a man, for it would destroy him from the inside. I had always kept that in mind, but looking at these young bucks with their zeal to end a war that hadn't even begun yet, a thought crossed my mind, one I intended to pass on to Pa. In their haste to get on with the fight, these lads didn't seem to have any fear at all. And that may be good for a show of bravado, but in the back of my mind I was wondering if Taylor and his boys had given any thought to what the Mexicans knew about us.

* * *

The sun gave off a blistering heat that morning, yet by noon Zach Taylor's little army had traveled a full five miles, equaling their distance of the previous day. By then those of us in the advance scouting party had reported sighting Mexican soldiers gathering ahead. But it didn't stop Old Rough 'n' Ready, and he continued to march an additional two miles into the middle of the afternoon. When he stopped, it was upon a spacious, grassy plain spotted with several freshwater ponds. Our destination was Fort Texas, across the Rio Grande, where five hundred men were awaiting our arrival, and we would have to cross the area in front of us now to get there.

When someone said the place was called Palo Alto, I didn't pay much attention. At the moment I could have cared less what it was called. What bothered me was the sight of those seven thousand enemy soldiers just a-sitting there waiting for a reason to fire on us.

"Too bad Andy Jackson ain't here," Ab said with a chuckle. "He'd have loved it."

"How's that?" I asked.

"At New Orleans, of course!"

Then I remembered Pa's stories of how Old Hickory and his backwoods frontiersmen had slaughtered the British as they marched into battle in full view of the enemy. Which was just what seemed to be taking place now.

As Rangers, we had been positioned apart from the regular force and now watched Taylor as he ordered his men to battle positions, placing his artillery batteries between his infantry regiments. The Mexican forces were backed by tall timber and a thick chaparral, which made the possibility of additional troops a threat, whereas Taylor and his men were standing out in the open with no cover at all. The whole situation almost seemed laughable, as though it were one of those old-fashioned duels I had read about. Or a reincarnation, in force, of the Hamilton-Burr duel of 1804.

"What do you think, Ab?"

"What do I think?" The big man slowly grinned and shook his head in disbelief. "Finn, I'd say a good

Comanche war party could've wiped out every one of these pilgrims, as long as it takes 'em to get in position.''

While Taylor was getting his men in formation, a gaudily dressed man on a fine black stallion appeared before the Mexican ranks, parading back and forth in front of his men, shouting what must have been words of encouragement. But it wasn't so much the man as it was the situation that caught my eye. Nathan and I had seen the very same thing at San Jacinto when Santa Anna had pulled the same type of daring antics. Recalling what Nathan had told me about seeing the same kind of show-offishness by some Comanche chief he had been trailing some years back, I was beginning to wonder if this sort of thing was getting to be fashionable or if it was simply done for us Callahans. It was enough to make a body think some. I'll say that.

"Don't look like they've changed an awful lot."

Suddenly the commander and his mount disappeared and there was a roar of a Mexican cannon. The grapeshot fell far short of the American lines and was returned by our own artillery, which, at first, proved ineffective. This was followed by continuous smoke and fire belching from the cannons of both sides. Twice I saw the telling effects of Taylor's artillery, once when a cannonball made a direct hit on a Mexican cannon and a second time when a shot landed among the soldiers standing stiff in the ranks, sending clothing, weapons and parts of what were once men scattering in all directions.

For the most part, it was nothing more than an artillery duel in which the American forces outshot the oversized force in front of them. Men in the ranks on both sides began milling about now, Taylor's men anxious to get into battle, those of the Mexican army unsure of whether to stand and die in the face of withering gunfire or retreat to the trees for safety.

I was checking the loads of my second Walker Paterson when one young volunteer made the remark that he wished there were an Indian raid someplace just so he'd have something to do.

"Sure don't seem like we're doing much but watching these people kill each other off."

"Can't wait to fight," Ab said to me, knowing we

were both thinking the same thing, that this youngster had never been in a good fight before.

Then, to everyone's surprise, a force of what seemed like hundreds of enemy soldiers came out of nowhere. They were a combination of infantry and slow-moving artillery pieces, but what worried me was the several hundred cavalrymen leading them. It might not have been so bad if they had rifles or even pistols, for the Mexican soldier seemed to have little luck with the proper firing of such artillery. But these men were carrying lances, and if there was one weapon a Mexican cavalryman could use effectively, it was a lance!

Right off you could see their objective was a sweeping flank attack on the supply wagons, but Taylor's right-flank infantrymen were already moving forward obliquely to the right to stop them. And it didn't take much to see that those advancing infantrymen would be cut to pieces by the Mexican cavalry charge.

"Sonny, you got your wish," Ab said to the youngster who was so eager for battle. Then, to the rest of the men, he said, "Make sure you got full loads, boys. 'Pears to me them fellas down there could use a hand." Then, pistol in hand, he waved it above his head and yelled, "Charge!"

There wasn't no more'n twenty of us, but each man had at least two Colt revolvers and knew he would have to make every shot count if he was going to come out of this alive. We rode toward those lancers at a full gallop, the only weapons being fired besides our own being those of the infantrymen as they outshot those Mexicans who did have rifles.

We were only thirty feet from the lancers when we opened fire. I fired twice, as fast as I could, sure I had downed two of the riders. But before the smoke could clear enough for a second volley, the damndest thing happened! Not a one of us expected it, but we had sure enough broken through their front line and were now inside of it, surrounded by what seemed to be an enemy that was as confused and angry as we were, if that was possible. What happened next took only a few seconds, but, lordy, were they long. And I'll tell you, hoss, I never would have taken Ab Sharpson to be much of a prayerful man, but he proved then and there that he knew when to turn to his Maker.

"Almighty God," he said, "be on our side if you can, but if you can't, for Christ's sake don't be on theirs. You stand off on one of these hills and just look, and you'll see the damndest fight you ever saw in your life." Then, instead of saying, "Amen," he yelled out, "Charge, boys, charge!"

I never was sure if it was Ab Sharpson, Sam Colt or the Almighty that got us through that scrape, but I suspicion it was a combination of the three. I let my mount know I still had heels and started firing both Colts as fast as I could at whatever was getting in my way. I was down to my last two shots when I felt something tear at my shirt, followed by a warm feeling at my side. I knew it was blood, but there was no time to check, so I let go those last shots and tucked the pistols back in my waistband, awkward as it was. Out of habit, I reached for the bowie knife at my side, for there were still men ahead of me before I'd be out of this mess. One of them had taken a real interest in me and was heading straight for me, lance at the ready. Now, that bowie knife may never be as big as a lance, but you can bet she's just as strong and just as dangerous, and I made sure that fella knew it. I tried parrying his weapon as best I could and brought the knife down across his shoulder, catching a glimpse of blood as he rushed on by.

Then everything seemed to stop as the Mexican force retreated and we regrouped. We had broken the attack! And, by God, we'd survived what seemed like certain death!

"I don't believe it, Ab," I said as we reined in back at the supply wagons. "We all got out alive."

"Yeah, we did," Ab said, then glanced over his shoulder at a riderless horse with a body slung over it. "Except him."

"Who was it?"

"The kid," he said sadly, adding, more to himself than anyone else, "They just can't wait to fight."

It was two more hours before the cannons stopped. And they did that only because of a brushfire that had started on the plain between the two forces because of the artillery fire. Taylor and his men had advanced far enough on the right side so that the Mexican forces were pinned up against the timber of the chaparral. The front lines had changed direction as much as a weather vane when the wind blows slowly from westerly to southwest. And that's where both forces found themselves at the end of that day.

Taylor had lost five men killed and fifty wounded, one of the dead being our Ranger. But according to reports, for every American who died that day, there had been one hundred Mexicans who also died on the battlefield. No one could tell how many we had wounded.

That side hit I'd felt was nothing more than a minor flesh wound. But that night it was hard to sleep, and only the exhaustion of the day forced me to nod off. Hearing the voices out in the dark like that, well, it gets down right spooky. I reckon that's why I'll never make a soldier. It's just too damn hard to lie there and try sleeping when all you can hear are the voices of wounded men still out there on the battlefield, crying out in agony . . . knowing that they're dying.

Chapter 4

I found out a long time ago that heroism on a battle-field is something they write about in the history books. Sort of like that Parson Weems and his biography of George Washington. Now, I don't doubt that Washington was a brave man, not at all. But I'll tell you, friend, I'd lay odds that when he was crossing the Delaware or fighting at Valley Forge or any other time during the Revolution, he wasn't thinking about what they'd put down in some history book about him. It never does happen that way. What a man does is go out and do what he has to, knowing there ain't nothing romantic about it and that at day's end he'll wind up either alive or dead. And if he's honest with himself he'll pray either that his death will be a quick and honorable one or, if he makes it through alive, that his wounds will be slight. I'd been in enough fights and seen enough men die slowly to know that I wouldn't want it any other way.

But it wasn't the wound I was aware of right off when I woke up the next morning. It was the smell of burnt grass and the start of what smelled like the stink of dead bodies out on that battlefield. It was past sunup and there was a lot to be done, but when I tried to move, I felt weak and could only sag back onto my bedroll.

"Looks like the fever broke," Ab Sharpson said, looking down on me. "Your wound must have got infected, son, 'cause you were tossing and turning all night."

Ab explained that they had just broken camp and Taylor and his men had gone on to pursue the Mexicans. The general had left behind his sick and wounded and an additional force to get his supply wagons back to Point

Isabel. To do so he had cut his fighting force from two thousand to seventeen hundred men, and I wondered if, after the fracas of the previous day, he might not be just a bit crazed his own self in going after an enemy of unknown size—again. And unless Ab knew something I didn't, it sure seemed like the Mexicans were more apt to get reinforcements than we were. When I wrinkled my nose at the increasingly horrid smell, Ab glanced out over the battlefield.

"Gotta give those boys credit," he said. When I frowned, he continued. "The medics. They worked all night on the wounded from *both* sides. Just now getting a breather, I reckon."

After a pause during which he spat out his chaw, he continued.

"The general sent Sam Walker and a few of his men out in front to scout this morning. It ain't that far to Fort Texas, and I reckon he figures he can make it there today without the supplies and such bogging him down."

"And," I said, "if he doesn't run into that Mexican outfit again."

Ab nodded, a look on his face that seemed to acknowledge what we both knew to be inevitable.

"By the way, Finn, I sent home a handful of boys this morning. They'd been hit bad enough not to be of much more use than to ride back to their own spreads, so I let 'em go. Just wanted to let you know, cause I know you got your family to meet back in St. Louis and all. So when you get to feeling better, I won't hold it against you if you ride out." Placing a hand on my shoulder, he squeezed it gently. "You done fine yesterday, Finn. I'm proud of you." Then he started fidgeting with his pockets as though he were looking for something but didn't know what. I had seen men do it before, men who had been through an experience with others and knew it was time to leave but found it hard. So they busied themselves, as though to make an excuse for delaying the departure. "Well, uh, you take care, boy. I've got to catch up with the rest."

Watching him leave, I could think of few men I would rather serve with than Ab Sharpson. The man was a loyal friend, and I would miss him.

By noon I had eaten and felt much stronger, although

there was still some pain in my side. A burial detail was working as fast as it could, but the smell of death grew stronger with each passing hour, and I decided to ride for a while to get the stiffness out of my body.

I wandered over the land toward the west. The whole area was spotted with water holes and closed-up bunches of chaparral. If anyone had been in that area, it had not been for some time, for there was hardly a trace of footprints or tracks of any sort. The day was again becoming hot, and the horse had smelled water, so I let him have his head. After he drank I followed the Rio Grande at an easy pace. It was silent, and it crossed my mind that Taylor must have reached his destination or I would surely have heard the cannonade between the two forces. I was trying to put the war out of my mind when I rode up behind a thicket of chaparral and thought I heard voices on the far side.

I dismounted, leaving the horse ground-tied, and moved in behind the thicket. When I pulled back a branch, I had to look twice to make sure I was seeing what I was seeing! It wasn't the sight of the three Mexican soldiers or the old man before them that I found hard to believe. What seemed like a mirage was the strongbox on the ground between them!

They were fifty yards off, so I couldn't hear everything they said, but it appeared that the old man had dug a hole and the three soldiers were now arguing with him over it. Were they digging up something? I had heard some of the numerous tales of lost Spanish treasure that abounded throughout this country and knew that there were as many men who believed in the stories as there were that disbelieved. And those who believed would spend a lifetime tracking down the treasures, just as those who didn't believe would scoff at them. But the strongbox I now saw looked like nothing I had ever heard described as carrying the riches of the conquistadors.

The bearded old man was pleading now, slowly backing up as one of the soldiers raised his rifle to him. I was out of range for an effective pistol shot, so it was the Hawken I nailed the soldier with. The shot shattered the silence, throwing a shock into the old man as well as the others as the rifleman fell dead. The two soldiers gave a quick look toward the thicket and were gone by the time I had reloaded my rifle.

"He is dead, señor," the old man said as I neared him. "You saved my life, señor, and I am grateful."

"Can't say as I ever took to bushwhacking a man," I said, rolling the dead man over with my boot. "But what's an old man like you doing here in the first place? You sure ain't no soldier," I added, taking in the simple cotton shirt and pants he wore. "You live here, do you?"

"I am Ramón, señor," he said, tipping his peasant's hat politely. "I am the ferryman for this part of the river. It was General Arista and his men that I ferried across the river not long ago.

"It took me three days to get the army over, crossing and crossing back, day and night. And, oh, señor." He smiled. "I had many desires to go with them. There was *musica* and the *banderas*—how you say—the flags, all bright in the air, and the men were all happy and singing. But I did not go, and in three days more here they were back, but without the *musica* or *banderas* and not needing any ferryboat. They came in flocks, running and crawling like the *tortugas*, the turtles, and they fell into the water flat on all fours like *tortugas* and never stopped till they were into Mexico.

"They had been in the fight, and I am glad now that I did not go with them. So many went so fast that they had no time to take the general's silver *platas* from which he ate. And they get me, señor. 'Instead of a ferry guide,' they say, 'We have another mission for you.' And I dig these," he said, spreading a hand over a twenty-foot expanse of riverbed.

"And what are these?" I glanced briefly at six holes that had been dug, refilled and tamped down as though to appear the same as the rest of the area.

"I don't know, señor." The old man shrugged, a smile forming at the corners of his mouth. "Gold, perhaps? The *tesoro* of the *conquistadores*? If you are a believer and it is gold you seek—"

"Reckon I'm not much of a believer, mister. Those stories are likely all somebody's imagination. But I wouldn't mind finding out what this stuff is, anyway."

I used the dead Mexican's rifle to beat the lock off of

the strongbox, ruining most of the rifle's working parts in the process. And when it opened, I reckon both that old man and I looked like we were about ready to drop our eyeballs. And I'll tell you, hoss, those tales of the lost Spanish treasures might have been imaginary, but what I saw before me now looked God Almighty real for a fact!

The strongbox was filled with gold coins in various denominations and looked more like a Mexican army payroll than any mythical lost treasure. Looking at the old man, I thought I saw the same look that must have been on my face, only with him it seemed like there was something holding him back. I remembered seeing Cooper Hansen going through a dead man's pockets after a fight and justifying it with a comment that they were the "spoils of war." Well, our cattle and ranch were gone now and someone had to pay for it, and any soldiers this payroll was meant for were probably dead. I was reaching down toward the contents of the box when I felt the old man's hand on my arm.

"No! You must not take it, señor!"

"A dead man don't need money, friend," I heard myself say as I scooped up a handful of coins and placed them in my shot pouch.

"But they say it brings death, señor. A curse. They say that whoever—"

"That's just another Indian story. You're being superstitious."

As I said it I bent down to pick up another handful of the gold. It was then the shot rang out. Some things are ingrained in a man, I reckon, and living long enough to tell about them is one of them. Out of habit I rolled to the side, dropping the coins and bringing up the Colt as I did. The shot had come from across the river, far enough away so that the Colt did little good. The Hawken lay on the other side of the strongbox and wouldn't have done much more by the time I got it, for all I saw was a man hastily mount his horse and gallop away.

"You all right, mister?" I asked, watching the rider flee. Then, glancing over next to the strongbox, I saw the lifeless body of the old man. He had been shot through the heart, probably dead before he hit the dirt. But of one thing I was sure: The shot had been meant for me. Whoever the rifleman was, he was a backshooter, and that made him about as deadly as any rattlesnake to my mind, for he would strike a second time if he missed the first.

I stripped the dead soldier of his shot pouch and filled it with more of the coins. Then I dug a shallow grave for the old man, buried him and began a second grave for the dead Mexican before deciding against it.

"Leave you for buzzard bait," I said to him and stuffed some more of the coins in my pockets. The hole had already been dug, so I pushed the strongbox into it and did a quick job of refilling it to make it look like the others.

There was something strange about the assassin that kept tugging at my mind. Or was it his horse? There was something there that could tell me just who it was who had tried to kill me.

I crossed the river and stopped where I thought I had seen the man. It didn't take long to find the tracks, for they were the only ones in the area. And when I saw them I knew who it was who had tried to sharpshoot me. More than one horse might have a loose shoe, but only one had a spotted buckskin rump like that of the horse I had seen ride away this afternoon.

I should have known. I had almost forgotten about him and I should have known.

There was the sound of the cannons to the south as I rode away, but I paid little attention to it. Right now I had my own war to fight.

I found him in the same area I had come from earlier. The doctors were still working to heal the wounded, and the burial detail was still busy. The stench was getting worse, but I didn't care. For the first time since leaving at noon I remembered my own wound, realizing that most of the stiffness was gone now. But it wouldn't have mattered anyway.

He was talking to three other men when I walked up behind him.

"Garvey."

I hit him with a roundhouse punch that sent him sprawling into the others as he turned around. The blow surprised him, and I landed two more solid hits, one to the chest, another to the nose, before I saw the defeat that always seemed to linger in the man's eyes. Garvey seemed unwilling or unable to get up and looked to the others for help. But the men he had been talking to were of the wounded and seemed in no mood for a fight. They wanted to get involved even less when I pulled out my bowie knife. Or maybe they could see the anger I was feeling and figured I was as capable of cutting them up if they interfered as I was of skinning Garvey. Real slow-like, I knelt down beside him on one knee. He was scared bad, but when I pulled a handful of his scalp back in one hand and placed the tip of my knife just below his chin, he turned sheet white.

"You're mad, Callahan!" There was a desperation in his voice now.

"That's right, Garvey. I'm mad. I get that way when people start shooting at me. Especially little weasels like you."

"I didn't try to—you can't prove anything!"

"That's right, Garvey. I can't prove anything. But no one rides a buckskin like yours, and no one is as greedy or cowardly as you." I pressed the tip of the knife into his chin, just enough for a trickle of blood to start flowing.

"Don't! Please! You'll kill me!"

"I ought to, Garvey. I ought to let you bleed to death right here and now." I got to my feet, wiped the blade off on my pants, placed it in its sheath. "I'm going now, Garvey, and I don't ever want to see you again. Understand? Because if I do, you'll bleed one hell of a lot more than you are now."

Chapter 5

"I tell you, Captain, I've got to find a courier to get this report to my newspaper!" I heard the man say. He was short and pudgy and sloppily dressed, one of those easterners who never get used to the climate out here and just flat refuse to change their ways. His dirty white shirt was soaked with sweat and his face had a terrible sunburn, the type gotten by one who is not used to spending long periods of time under a torturous sun. "Are you sure you can't spare a man?"

"I'm sorry, sir, but our men are all committed," the young captain said. "You may be writing the war, Mr. Sanders, but we're fighting it. Those are the general's orders."

"Hell, I might as well send in a letter of resignation," Sanders said to no one in particular.

I didn't know the easterner, but it didn't take much to figure out who the young officer talking to him was. As short a time as we had been there, it didn't take long to hear about Captain William W. S. "Perfect" Bliss, the assistant adjutant general to Zach Taylor himself. Sam Walker had served under Taylor in the Seminole Wars and mentioned that other than letter writing, the general hated the administrative aspect of soldiering, considering himself more a fighting man than a pencil pusher. In its wisdom the Army had assigned "Perfect" Bliss to be Taylor's adjutant, and the two were said to get along fine considering that they were complete opposites. Bliss was a bright young West Pointer who did things by the book (hence the nickname "Perfect") and would likely have received the scant respect Sam said Taylor had for such junior-grade officers if he hadn't been so useful. Taylor, on the other hand, was the original Indian fighter who relied on his instincts to stay alive more than he ever would any book on warfare. So the young captain made up for what the general lacked, many times writing out his directives for him.

"Maybe I can help you out, mister," I said to the easterner, Sanders. "Which way you headed?"

A glimmer of hope crossed the man's face. "New Orleans, and there's twenty dollars in it for you."

I frowned. New Orleans was a bit out of the way of the destination I had in mind.

"I'll double it!" The man was obviously desperate for a rider.

"Hold on a minute, mister. I've got something else to take care of first." Then I turned my attention to the officer. "You seen Captain Walker and his Rangers around of late?"

After the incident with Garvey, my immediate thought was to get out of the area as quickly as possible in case the man's friends showed up. But then I remembered the cannonade I had heard on the ride into camp and decided to see if there indeed had been another battle. If there had, I knew good and well old Sam Walker would have found a way into it. Besides, you don't leave your friends without saying good-bye.

"The last I heard, he was down on the *resaca* with his men."

"Resaca?"

"Resaca de La Palma. One of the prisoners says that is the name of the battlefield we fought on this afternoon."

"How did it go?"

"We whipped them soundly, sir, soundly." Bliss smiled. "In fact, I believe your Captain Walker and his men were at the fore." The captain gave me directions on where to find Walker, and the newspaperman, Sanders, once again began plying me.

"Look, bud, I've got to get this out of here, so can you make it quick?"

"What happened to your courier?"

"The damn fool decided he wanted to be a volunteer instead of a rider, and left."

I began walking my horse toward the scene of the battle, the reporter tagging along next to me.

"New Orleans ain't exactly where I'm headed."

"Where, then?"

"St. Louis. Got a family to meet there."

"Sixty bucks! And a passage," he huffed, out of breath or excited; I wasn't sure which. "I'll get you passage on one of the riverboats to St. Louis."

I was silent for a moment, remembering the small fortune I had found that afternoon.

"Tell you what, friend," I said. "You keep your money and your riverboat ticket. Just write a note to your boss telling him to have a fresh horse ready for me when I get there." I paused a moment before continuing. "And a meal, a good hot one."

"Say, mister, that's pretty generous! Saving me all that money like that." The man seemed amazed at the offer I'd made.

"Not really," I said, reining in my mount. "The way I look at it, you're gonna spend even more money trying to find a rider tomorrow if you don't today. All I'm doing is keeping you from getting fired today instead of tomorrow. Now, why don't you get whatever it is I'm supposed to be carrying ready and I'll meet you at Captain Bliss's tent in half an hour." Then I tugged on the reins and headed for the battlefield. "Right now I've got a friend to say so long to."

As it turned out, Sam Walker and his boys were the first ones to get into that fight, the way he explained it. Seems they had walked into an ambush.

General Arista and his men were gone that morning, and the feeling was that they had high-tailed it back down south. But Arista had gathered his forces, along with three hundred reinforcements, and positioned them on the Resaca de La Palma, a shallow ravine that had once been part of the ever-changing Rio Grande. The area was thick with chaparral, and his men had gathered deadwood and dried-up bushes and stacked them to fill any openings there might be. Arista knew he had us outnumbered and must have figured it wouldn't take no time to beat us.

As the advance scouting patrol, Sam and his Rangers

were the first to draw fire from the *resaca*. None of them were hit, but they damn sure knew they were in for one hell of a fight. Once Taylor found out about it, he had his artillery moved up the road and put in position, along with his infantry. What followed did turn out to be "natural hell" on the Rio Grande.

The battle lasted for over an hour but was anything but an artillery duel. According to Sam, the infighting was some of the worst he had ever seen, men clubbing each other to death or going for each other's throats with everything from bayonets to bowie knives. Finally, the Mexicans broke and ran. They were figuring they had killed some twelve hundred Mexicans when I got there and found Sam Walker.

"Looks like I won't have to write that letter to Sam Colt after all, Finn," he said after explaining how the battle had gone. "I think somehow or other this general figures I'm some kind of hero, although I'll be damned if I know why."

"That so." I knew full well that Sam, like many a man out here, wasn't the type to brag about his exploits, no matter how heroic they might have been.

"So he says. Fact is, he's talking about sending me back East to do some recruiting for his army. And if he does that, I'm sure gonna make time to stop in and see Sam Colt again. The general says that the year he's been out here, his men have spoken well of the Colt Paterson and want more of them. And Jack Hays is convinced he can get the backing for enough money to purchase a thousand of them for his Rangers."

"But I thought he only had five hundred men that volunteered."

"He does," Sam said, smiling. "He's wanting two for each man."

I let out a long, low whistle.

"Giving a man that kind of firepower could make him overconfident! Especially if Sam modifies that Walker Paterson the way you're talking about."

Sam laughed.

"Could be, Finn, but I know that if I can get the Rangers to believe in it, I can get Colt a contract with the Army, too."

"Well, luck to you, Sam," I said, shaking his hand.

"I've got to git. Seems there's a nervous fella here that's got some kind of news to get to a paper, and I'm riding it for him."

"Where to?"

"New Orleans. But then I'm heading up to St. Louis. Nathan's supposed to be bringing Ma and Pa back down our way, and I'm afraid we don't have much to go back to. Listen, you say howdy to Sam Colt for me, and tell him I want a couple of those revolvers when he gets 'em made."

"Sure thing, Finn."

Sanders was waiting for me at Bliss's tent. He handed me the report, the address it was to be taken to and the note I had requested. I gulped down a quick cup of coffee and mounted up.

"Mister," I said, looking down at the nervous little man, "I'm glad you've got your job."

"Oh? And why do you say that?"

" 'Cause I don't think I could stand it." I studied him again, slowly shook my head. "If I had a job that made me feel half as worried as you look . . . well, friend, I do believe I'd have a soured stomach by now."

Then I reined the horse north, dug my heels into his side and headed for New Orleans.

Chapter 6

I made it to New Orleans in just over twenty-four hours. But I'll tell you, friend, I wasn't at all sure that horse was going to go much further. So instead of asking directions to this newspaper office I was heading for, I took him straight to the livery and undid everything on him. The boy minding the livery looked like he figured the horse was going to die any minute, the way he was blowing. I reckon that was another one of those moments when I got to wondering why a man did what he did to run good horseflesh into the ground.

"Son," I said to the lad, "if he ain't dead tired, he ought to be. I know I would be if I'd carried him as far as he has me." When the boy slowly smiled, I added, "Give him double of everything and treat him good."

"Ain't no other way, mister," the lad said, but his eyes were focused on the gold piece I'd placed in the palm of his hand. He was still staring at it when I asked him for directions to the office I was looking for and threw the *mochilas* over my shoulder.

It wasn't really an office, at least not compared to the huge buildings surrounding it. It looked more like a temporary structure with a one-door entrance/exit that had been stuck in between two fair-size buildings and likely had a hell of a long alley way behind it. The fella inside was even less impressive, and about as short-tempered as the newspaperman I had run into down on the Rio Grande.

"Now, where the hell have you been?" the man said as soon as I walked through the door. It was almost as if he knew who I was and what I was there for. When I squinted at him, he only held out an impatient hand, adding, "Well, come on, what have you got?"

"No wonder you can't keep any riders, mister. I don't see how anyone could stand being around anyone with as *pleasant* a personality as you have."

"Come on, mister. You're wasting my time" was his only reply, the stern hand still firmly in place.

I reached inside my buckskins, pulling out a sheaf of papers that had been rolled and given to me before leaving Texas. For safekeeping I had stuck them inside my shirt and under one arm so they wouldn't come loose. And as uppity as this fella was getting, I had a pure notion of either pulling out my bowie or the Colt and planting it in that hand of his. But just watching him grimace as I reached inside my shirt was going to be pleasure enough. And if the papers had a bit of sweat on them, well, I couldn't think of anyone who deserved it more right then than this fella.

"Don't they ever teach you people to bathe?" he asked in a disgusted voice as he gingerly took the papers in hand. Or maybe it was seeing me smile that did it.

"Sure," I said, my grin spreading. "But first they taught us to care for the horses and those with us." I shrugged. "Water's scarce, so we usually wait for a flash flood to fill up the river before getting out the lye soap. You know how it is."

But he didn't. He had that incredible look of disbelief a body has after hearing a tall tale, only this fella was going to swallow it as gospel and probably print it up in one of his editions. Not that what I was telling him was all that far from the truth, but if this man had ever been in a flash flood, he'd know damn well it wasn't the place to be tending to your armpits.

He read the papers through quickly then handed them to a lean, short lad, who I took to be the next rider who would carry them on to wherever they were going from here. As soon as they were in his hand, the lad was gone.

"Speaking of being took care of," I said, reaching into my pocket, "that fella down Texas way said you'd take care of a few things for me."

He studied the paper a minute, then chuckled to himself. "Mister, you'll be lucky to get the price of a meal from this outfit." When he saw the look on my face, he stopped laughing. "Look, this guy tells all of his riders that. Hell, he'll do anything to get someone to ride for him!"

"Mister," I said, trying to sound a bit more patient than I was feeling and not succeeding at all, "I've been without sleep for damn near two days. I've been in the saddle for a full day riding hell-for-leather to get that lousy piece of paper from one ungrateful person to another. And I just put out a good chunk of money to get my horse taken care of." I leaned over the counter then, placing my right hand loosely on the butt of the Colt. "So, *friend*," I said, emphasizing the word, "you'd do well to come up with *at least* the price of a good meal and a place to bunk, or . . ." And here I paused a few seconds to let my words sink in. At the same time I tightened the grip on my Colt and continued in a hard, even voice. "Or I won't be calling you *friend* anymore." The implication was that I'd be calling him dead, but I wouldn't have done that to the man. Nathan might have, but I had always figured to have more patience than my older brother. Besides, I had a whole mochilaful of those gold pieces, so it wasn't a matter of not being able to pay for my supper. I reckon I just never got used to blustery types like this one having their way.

"Well now, friend," he said in a nervous voice, trying as hard as you please to act like he was an agreeable sort. "You happen to be in luck today. Yes, sir, you surely do," he added, reaching into his pocket and extracting a five-dollar piece. "That'll get you a decent meal and a bunk overnight." Then, sniffing the air as though it were tainted, he said, "And a bath, if you'd like."

I pocketed the money, knowing full well I wasn't the cleanest-looking man in town by any means and intending to get washed up as soon as I could. But my stomach was telling me that piece of beef jerky I had a couple of days back wasn't going to last much longer.

"First things first," I said. "Point me in the direction of one of those places that'll serve up a good meal."

He rattled off some fancy name that I figured I'd remember as long as it took me to find the place, and I headed for it, taking in the city on my way.

Riding in, I hadn't taken much time to look for any-place but the livery and that newspaper office, but it was a half-dozen blocks according to the directions I had to the eatery I was looking for, so I took in the fancy settings that were making up the town of New Orleans. And let me tell you, hoss, it wasn't nothing like Texas . . . or Hartford, for that matter. The houses were two and three stories, most all of them made out of brick or sandstone of some sort or another. Walking along, I'd ask directions once in a while and take notice of the street names as well. Some of the buildings had a touch of New England to them and were built in the form of what they were calling row houses, or townhouses, as some said. Oh, they were English, all right, for it was hard to miss the numerous squared-off, oblong windows guarded by shutters, that only an Englishman could tolerate. I never could understand that about them, the English. The way they kept to themselves as a people, acting as if the only part of them the rest of the world would never know was their politics. Strange.

There was another residential block I passed called Charles Street. When I asked about the houses, I was told the street was also known as Architects' Row, since the structures there had been Anglo in concept but with a bit of the French and Greek thrown in, resulting in arched doorways rather than the square English entrances. I remembered reading about how some of those Greeks were excellent architects as well as philosophers and athletes and . . .

Sometimes you can be thinking to yourself, reminisc-ing or just pondering something, when a fact will fall on you as hard as a Comanche war party when you're out on the prairie by your lonesome. And when it does, it seems so obvious to you that you could cuss yourself for being so stupid as to overlook it. With Nathan it would be the fanatical dedication he had to his weapons, al-ways keeping them cleaned and ready for a fandango in case someone wanted to start the ball. But with me, well . . .

"Damn!" I must not have said it under my breath, for I found myself apologizing to a couple of ladies walking by in the opposite direction.

Then I just stood there, dumbfounded, asking myself

how I could have forgotten! It hadn't hit me until just then, remembering about those Greeks and all, but by God, I'd forgotten all about my books!! What with the massacre of Homer Johnston and his family and then the burning of our own place and the chaos and fighting that had followed when we took off and fought those Mexicans, I had clean forgotten about the couple, three dozen books I had in the house!! Oh, they could most of them be replaced, but a lot of them were hard to come by and would be hard to find out here. It was enough to make a body sick to his stomach when he lost something that meant as much to me as those books did.

I didn't pay much attention afterward to the houses and such, just looking up occasionally to see if my directions were still right. Somehow the realization that I was without those books made me feel worse than I had at the sight of all that work we had put into our ranch going to waste like that as it burned. It was almost like being alone in the world, which is maybe why I didn't see him at first.

"Now, don't tell me things is that bad off, sonny."

When I looked up, I saw a grizzled older man who appeared to have a few teeth missing on one side of his mouth. He wasn't all that big, hunching over like a man who makes a life at riding herd on his cattle when the weather is inclement. He wore a western hat made out of beaver and a fringed buckskin jacket, but that was all that was western about him. His trousers were those of a city man and were stuffed into the tops of a shiny pair of black boots.

"Who's asking?" I wasn't feeling all that hospitable and, like it or not, it showed.

"Dean. Sam'l Dean," he said, smiling and sticking out a paw. When I shook it but didn't reply, he paused a moment, as though not sure of what to do next, then asked, "Where you heading?"

"Put some food in my stomach if I can find the eatery," I said and mentioned the fancy-named restaurant.

"Oh, that's jess a couple blocks and a bit south of here, son," he said, nice as you please. "Say, I never did get your name."

"Callahan. Finn Callahan." If it sounded gruff it was because I still wasn't in the mood for company.

"Where you from?" he asked after a while.

"Why do you ask?"

"Shoot, boy, ain't no one but me and another plains-man would wear that kind of garb in this town," he said, eyeing my getup. And from what I had seen so far I would have to agree with him. This New Orleans was one of those new civilized places where a body was expected to go around in his Sunday-go-to-meeting clothes all the rest of the days of the week, too.

"Come outta Texas."

"Where you headed?" he asked excitedly.

"Same place, in a roundabout way, I reckon."

I wasn't all that keen about giving out any more infor-mation about myself than I had to to a stranger, but as it turned out, this Dean fella was a transplanted western man who couldn't break the habit of the old ways, or so he said.

"I jess find someone who's a-passing through from out yonder and see can I catch up on what's going on out there."

So I talked mostly in generalities as we walked, filling him in on what I knew firsthand about this Mexican fandango we had gotten into and such like that.

When we got to the restaurant it only took one glance from the outside to see I'd likely have trouble getting to the inside. I could see through the glass front windows that whoever it was that made up the late-afternoon crowd was what you'd call pretty smart dressers. Coats with long tails and fancy vests and dresses like I had only heard Ma talk of one day having. Dressed as I was, it crossed my mind that the newspaperman had sent me here apurpose just to embarrass me. But getting in didn't seem to be a problem at all for Sam'l Dean. He walked right in, and the headwaiter nodded politely to him, then drew up short when I took a step inside.

"He's my guest," Dean said in what I could only take to be a false uppity manner. For a moment the two were giving each other a hard stare. Then Dean broke it when he shook his head in disbelief. "This is Pee-Air, Calla-han," he said, contorting the man's name emphatically. "Would you believe he ain't been a day in his life without a bar of soap and hot water?"

"Can't say as I blame him," I said, trying to keep as

straight a face as I could. "I've seen a couple of under-takers dressed like him that had to take second jobs 'cause they couldn't drum up the business." Then, lean-ing a bit closer to the waiter, I whispered, "You do carpentry work, too, do you?"

"This way, please" was all he said as he led us to a table.

Now, you've got to understand that this place was like nothing they had in Texas that I ever seen. These people had never heard of community tables, nosiree. Why, they had little tables that were squared-off even that could hardly fit one man and a good-size meal, much less four people for the chairs at the table. And the silverware was like the good stuff Ma had that she got out for company or special occasions, not the flimsy tin pieces we had at our ranch.

We took our seats and I pulled off my hat and set it on the far side of the table. That was when this Frenchman started sounding like he had something in his throat, on purpose. So I put my hat on the chair and he started acting the same way. Then, underneath my breath I said, "To hell with you, bud," and sloshed it on my head and just pushed it back a mite.

When the waiter asked if we'd like anything to drink, Dean ordered two ryes. "They wouldn't think of serving bar whiskey in a place like this," he said, adding in a confidential voice, as though he were telling me a secret, "That way they can charge two bits a shot." That was about four or five hours' worth of work out in can-see, can't-see country, for wages weren't quite up to a dollar a day back then. "But I fixed 'em," the man continued, his face and eyes taking on a mischievous look. And when the waiter brought our drinks, I saw what he meant, for they didn't come in regular shot glasses. These glasses were just shy of what you'd call goblets! Well, I knew good and well that if I chugalugged that much of anything that had a kick to it on my empty stomach, I'd likely pass out from shock, so sipping was all I was up to about then. But this Dean fella knocked it back like it was part of his system and told the Frenchman he'd take another.

"And would monsieur like another drink also?"

"No thanks," I said, "I'll just let this one age a bit.

But I'll tell you what I could use, friend." The man raised a suspicious eyebrow, and I wasn't sure if it was because he didn't expect more than a few grunts and groans from an out-of-place heathen like me or if he'd never been called "friend" in his life. Odds were it was the last. "You serve beef here?"

"*Oui*, monsieur."

"Well, how about serving up a few thick slabs for me."

"*Oui*, monsieur."

"And one thing, friend," I said, catching his sleeve as he turned to leave. "Pan-fry 'em."

"Pan-fry them?" The man looked about as perplexed as I was feeling about this whole situation.

"Yeah. Burn it. Cook it well-done." When he gave me a glance that said I must be mad, I said, "Look, mister, just cook it so's it don't bite back or look like something I shot out on the trail a week back."

Dean was taking it all in with a certain amount of pleasure as the waiter turned a little green around the gills, then left. When he made no further attempt to interrogate me, I got to wondering about him.

"Tell me something, old-timer," I said, taking a sip of the rye, which didn't taste bad at all. "How is it you rate all this attention? Hell, from the waist up you look the same as me."

"Got me a job," he said, a certain proudness in the way he spoke. "Doing odds and ends for a lady here in the city."

"You're working for a *woman*?" I asked. If I sounded a bit taken back, it was because in those days women seldom did more than take care of a household and bear and raise the children. Those that were widowed or who never married generally took jobs as schoolteachers if they were educated, or maybe worked at directing a choir if they had an interest in religion. But rarely were they expected—or allowed—to do anything else with their life. But a lot of that belief came from the Calvinist religion on the Eastern Seaboard and, although strictly adhered to for the most part there, was more often than not modified or totally forgotten once a body got past the Ohio Valley. And this being New Orleans, well, I reckon it was just possible that those beliefs were different here as well.

"Oh, I know it ain't much to brag on, but it's honest work," he said. "That it is." Then, pondering a moment, he added, "Not like some of 'em that works for the painted ladies and such."

"Probably uglier than sin, too," I said in passing as the food came.

The beef was done as I had requested, although I thought I saw the waiter grimace as I dug into it. When he asked me if I was ready for another drink, I told him the one I had was still aging and to bring me some coffee. I was halfway through the pile of beef when I noticed that the plate had a side of rice and red beans, a concoction I'd not had before. It was spicy and had a good flavor to it, I decided.

"This town is just full of surprises, ain't it?" I said when I finished the rest of my coffee and took a swallow of what was left of my drink.

"Oh, it is, son, it is," Dean said, and I knew he was fixing to have some more fun, likely at someone else's expense. He then ordered the both of us another drink, saying, "He's gonna need it," to the waiter as the man left. When I frowned at him, he said, "Callahan, you see that table over there a row or two away?"

I half glanced in the direction he indicated, not really interested in whatever it was the old man had in mind. The whiskey had added that much more warmth to the food in my stomach, and at the moment the only thing I was thinking about was finding a bathhouse and a place to lay my body down after I cleaned up. As spiffied-up as the people were in this place, I didn't figure it would be long before someone reported me as being a vagrant and I'd be invited to leave town.

"That's the uglier-than-sin lady I work for."

When I looked again it was a stare more than a short glance that I took. Then I finished off the rest of my first drink and didn't even notice the waiter bring the second drink as Dean said, "Told you he'd need it." And I didn't really care just then.

She was the most beautiful woman I had ever seen!

She wore one of those fancy dresses I was getting used to seeing and sat ramrod straight in her chair. And if that didn't come from being some sort of schoolteacher, well, hoss, I'll eat my hat and snakeskin band on it! Her black hair was piled up somehow on the back of her head, and though I couldn't see her eyes across the twenty feet that separated our tables, I was betting they were as black as her hair. But she looked none too happy as she conversed in hushed tones with the man sitting across from her.

"Who's her friend?" I asked Dean, not taking my eyes from the lady's table. Whoever her friend was, he was a pure businessman, for he had on the formal suit and vest I recalled seeing back in Hartford that was the daily attire of those men who ran the community.

"One of the local bankers hereabouts."

Then of a sudden the two rose and I could see that although the banker was no more than average in height, he had been living the good life too long and a potbelly was beginning to bust open the bottom buttons on his vest. And the woman, well, she was about as tall as Ellie and had a right handsome figure to boot—at least what you could see of it for all the frills and such.

The crowd had thinned out by now, and there weren't but one or two other tables being waited on, but that didn't stop the banker from speaking loud enough for all to hear.

"I'm afraid I must insist on the payment within two weeks, Miss Talliafero." Then a smile that turned into a sneer came to his face as he added, "Or, if you wish, I could spread our little secret around. I'm sure many of the good people of this community would love to hear about it."

I don't think she liked that last piece, not atall. Fact is, I *know* she didn't like it! She made that pretty clear when the flat of her hand struck out as quick as a rattler and smacked against the clean-shaven banker's face. The sound it produced was right up there with the kind you hear from a well-worn bullwhip. And seeing a woman move as fast as that sort of makes a body not want to get on her bad side.

The two of them had the attention of everyone in the place by then, and I thought I saw a bit of a mist come over that banker's eyes. You know what I mean, the kind that goes with a sting that sticks with a person when they've done wrong and know it but won't admit it. That's the kind of look this fella had. But you can be sure that right behind that mist was a vengeful set of eyes that stared at her in one dead moment of silence.

"You get many fights hereabouts?" I asked Dean, not taking my eyes off the other two.

"Nah," the man said in disgust, "these people think they's too civilized for that." Then, out of the corner of my eyes, I saw that mischief come into his face again as he said, "Why, is they gonna be a fight?"

"Like you said, friend, this town's full of surprises," was all I said as I pushed back my chair and started toward the two.

"Perhaps *now* would be a good time to tell everyone about—"

It was that banker running off at the mouth again, but he never did finish that sentence, for that was when this lady slapped him hard again, just like she had a bullwhip in her hand and was dealing with a stubborn jackass. I had a feeling just then that this fella had about run out of patience and was ready to do some swinging of his own. Still, if these people ran to civilization, there were always other ways. I was just hoping that she wouldn't be taking another swing at him, for if he ducked this time, I'd be the one who'd wind up getting hit.

I must have looked a sight to them, wearing those greasy buckskins and all. And I hadn't removed the hat perched on the back of my head yet either, but that would come soon. You'd have thought they had given up the fighting and called a truce the way they were both staring at me as I neared them.

"How do, folks," I said, giving them my best smile but looking at the man while I talked.

"What the—"

"Looks like storm clouds gathering," I said, still looking at the man and now hearing several chuckles of laughter from those in the background as both he and the woman looked at me like I was mad. He was standing to my left, and I wanted to make sure I did it right. That was when I looked at the woman, trying to act as though I hadn't noticed her, something that was damn hard to do, and said, "Oh, pardon me, ma'am." Then like I'd seen those gentlemen do, and like I figured they'd want it done down here, I began to take my hat off and bow before her. Except I did it left-handed. I had taken a short step back so as to allow for room to bend over whilst I made my bow, at the same time sticking my foot right behind that banker's. Then, when I brought the hat off, it wound up in the man's face about the same time I leaned into him enough to send him falling. He fell with a thud, and I had a feeling he might have settled the building an inch or two. His face got red as he reached across his chest inside his coat. I stuck a boot atop his arm, pinning it to his chest and making him breathe a bit harder before he could say or do anything.

"Fella I knew one time said a man oughtn't talk about horsemanship lest he knows horses," I said evenly. "Don't seem to me you know much about manners or women, so maybe you'd better leave the lady alone."

The man seemed stunned at what I'd said as Pierre, the waiter, came over and helped him to his feet. He seemed about as rattled as the banker.

"Please, monsieur," he said in a pleading voice, "there will be no fighting in here?"

"Not unless he chooses to," I said, never taking my eyes from the banker. He had something inside his coat, and I was betting it wasn't a wallet either. Still, if he wanted to show it . . .

"And if I do?" the man said, regaining some of his bravado.

"Then I reckon Pee-Air here'll have him a chance to roast a pig," Dean said with a toothless grin. When the banker glanced at me and then his vest, the old man added, "Now Mr. Esquire, you don't want to do that. You know good and well a man don't live to be a hundred and five by doing foolish things."

"Certainly not" was his reply as he straightened his coat and abruptly turned and left.

The onlookers had begun to settle back in their seats while a couple of young boys who had seen it all through the front doors ran down the streets, relaying the story.

"Say, that friend of yourn give out some good advice 'bout horses and such," Dean said. "What'd you say his name was?"

"Socrates," I said, but I wasn't looking at him.

"Socra-who?" When I didn't reply he said, "Son, you need a drink." A few moments went by and he muttered to himself, "Well, I sure do."

I felt as out of place as I looked, fumbling with my hat and trying to look calm while I took in the girl before me. I was right about the eyes; they were as black as her hair. And to look at her in that dress, well, she was what Nathan would call . . . healthy. If you know what I mean. And a pretty face that looked like it had been taken care of real good, for there was nary a line on it. Or maybe that was because she was still young.

"I don't believe it," she said in a pleasant voice that seemed to fit her. "A man in buckskins who can quote Socrates."

"I never figured a man was ignorant just because he was dirty," I said. "If that were the case, I could think of Indians and whites alike who would have wound up dead a long time ago." I had no idea of what she was like other than the tough side I had just seen, so I just kept the conversation straightforward.

I was waiting for her to say something else about my way of dressing, but there was a long silence, and I was wondering if she was getting as short on words as I was.

"Well," she finally said, the smile still a pleasant one, "I imagine I should thank you for acting so gallant." She said that last just like I'd read it in those books, and it was then I knew for certain she was a teacher of sorts.

"Wasn't no acting to it. Just a matter of respect." When she said nothing, I felt the red creeping up the back of my neck and added, "Besides, I didn't want to get on your bad side." Her smile widened, and I heard a deep-throated laugh come from her as she offered her hand.

"I'm Talliafero. But please call me Tally."

"Pardon the dirt, ma'am," I said, taking her hand in mine and thinking I hadn't felt anything that soft in some time. "I'm Finn Callahan."

Then something strange happened inside me. I'd read all of those books, the Scott books that were romantic adventures where the fair damsel in distress would get saved; hell, I'd even envisioned how I'd act one day if I did something like that. But I just couldn't think of the right words! Or any words! Or maybe it was ten years of living the hard life that had made me skittish about meeting a person like this woman and feeling skin that soft. All I knew was that I had to get the hell out of there. I had done my good deed and now it was time to go. It was nothing that I or Nathan or any other frontiersman wouldn't have done if the situation arose, but here I was feeling like a fool and knowing I was out of place and had to git.

"You'll pardon me, ma'am, but I've got to settle up with this fella about my meal and be going." I turned right when I finished speaking, not wanting to give her a chance to say anything.

I tossed the five-dollar piece on the table, and Pierre said it would cover the drinks and the meal, which was more than I had figured. Dean stood silently, finishing his drink.

"Where will you go?"

Her voice startled me as I turned to see her again. Walking up behind a man ain't the thing to do where I come from, and I would normally have cussed a blue streak at anyone who did that. But she made me feel so damn helpless the way she spoke, sounding like she had real concern in her voice.

"Yeah," Dean said, swallowing the last of the contents of his whiskey glass, "you never did say jess where you was going. Here, I mean."

"I thought I'd find someplace that had enough water and soap to get all of what's on me off," I said, "and then find a bunk to sleep in."

"Nonsense." It was the woman speaking again, this time a sound of authority in her voice. She sure seemed to be changeable; I'll give her that. "You must come to my house. It is the least I can do to repay you. The hotels and bathhouses in this town will charge you three times their normal price."

"She's right," Dean said, nodding his head.

"Besides," she smiled, "it's been a long time since I've had an escort."

"Oh, don't you worry about that, Miss Tally," the old man chuckled, giving me a glance. "Ain't nobody sees something as grizzly as this gonna bother you on the streets."

*　　*　　*

You could see the Mississippi River from her house, a plantation type that was upriver from the center of town. It must have sat a good hundred feet off the main walk, but the distance in between was filled with shrubs that were clipped in what I had heard called the French Colonial manner. The house itself was made of sturdy wood painted white. It was a two-story affair with the second floor looking as if it were designed the same as the first—at least from the outside. There was a balcony on the second floor and the roof peaked in the center, with two protrusions called "hip roofs" on each side of it. Being that close to the river and with what I had heard about the fickleness of the Mississippi and how its banks tended to swell, the first thing that crossed my mind on seeing it was why it hadn't been swept away yet.

"Fancy, huh?" Dean said, eager to please.

"Beats a wikiup or a hogan, I reckon." But when I said it I got the impression he was a bit disappointed at my enthusiasm—or lack of it. But if he was the "used to was" frontiersman that he claimed, he should have known that I was just too damned tired to go rattling on about anything. Or maybe it was because I was more interested in this Miss Tally or Talliafero or whatever her name was. Walking on the outside of the walk, I found myself taking in her features again more than I was the fancy houses I made out to be looking at. And I made up my mind then and there that I was going to do a bit more conversing with this young lady.

What passed for a bathroom was near as big as some cabins I had seen on the frontier. The maid set to boiling some water for me while Talliafero disappeared for a few minutes, returning with a cloth shirt and pants. Stripping off those buckskins felt good about then, for a part of my shirt had been permanently stuck to my side from the blood that had caked there after that lancer had tried doing me in. As I slipped into the wooden tub, I noticed that the wound, which had opened some on the ride to New Orleans, now appeared to have closed again. And if Dean hadn't stayed there and kept a-talking, I do believe I would have fallen asleep right then; the hot water felt that good.

But when I finished, Dean excused himself to eat

supper, and not wanting to disturb anyone else in the house, I took to wandering around some. Not far from the entrance was a side room I had noticed earlier with a door slightly ajar. When I pushed it open, I made a mental note to talk to the woman about taking out a loan, for the room—and it, too, was large—contained nothing but wall-to-wall books! There were books by Shakespeare, Byron, Keats and Shelley, Dickens and many more I hadn't even heard of! And the more I looked, the more I found myself gauging how much time I had before having to meet Nathan and the rest of the family in St. Louis . . . and how much I could get read before then.

I pulled out a book I hadn't seen before titled *The Three Musketeers*, by an Alexander Dumas, and sat down to read.

And that was when I fell asleep.

Chapter 7

I woke up in a bed that had to be the softest thing I had ever slept in in my life. The trouble was, the only thing I was dressed in was my hide! My shirt and pants were draped over a chair a few feet away, and my hat was on a nightstand next to the bed. I threw back part of the covers and stuck out a leg, reaching for my hat as I did.

"Samuel said you'd do that."

Now, I've never taken to being surprised like that, and in any other situation I would have had one of those Colts of mine trained on whoever was talking before they had finished being long-winded. But I sure must have looked the fool right then, for I slapped on that hat and got a good case of tangle-foot of the arms, my right arm reaching for one of the pistols on the nightstand, the other desperately reaching for those covers I had thrown back! But when I heard her deep-throated laugh, I sort of slowed down and started turning a beet-red, for I knew I had nothing to fear from the girl Talliafero.

"He said you westerners dressed from the top down," she said, leaning to the side and taking a look at my bare leg. I don't know why, but a man gets to be self-conscious about things like that. Or maybe it's because he figures he's the one who's supposed to be doing the looking. I pulled my leg back, banging it into the sideboard of the bed, letting out a cuss word as I did. If it bothered the woman, she didn't let on. Instead she smiled again, amused at my situation. Funny thing was, I didn't seem to mind her at all, even as awkward as I was feeling right then. "I'll have the maid set another place for supper," she said.

"Supper?"

"Why, yes," she said incredulously. "You've been asleep for close to twenty-four hours, you know."

With that she left, and I dressed in the clothes I found there, remembering the book in her library and having sat down with it. When I finished dressing, I automatically reached for the Colt and its holster, then remembered where I was and thought better of it, leaving the weapon and hat on the stand.

The dining room was set up just as fancy as the eatery I had been in the day before except that the table was a bit longer and could seat maybe half a dozen people. The food was served, and we ate in silence for a while, me and Miss Talliafero and Sam'l Dean. She wasn't dressed up fancy this time, wearing the common type of cotton dress that I had seen on the frontier. Those fancy dresses I had seen most of the women wearing in this town might be fine for showing off or those shindigs they all went to, but they sure didn't show much of the woman for all the hoops and underthings and such. These cotton dresses now, well, at least a body could see a woman's ankles if nothing else, and this woman's were right pretty.

I hardly noticed Dean during that time, focusing my attention more on the food and the woman. After she had mentioned how long I had slept, my stomach began to growl and I knew she wasn't joshing me. The only conversation came about when I asked for my clothes and was told that they had been burned, boots and all!

"Some evenings I take a walk," she said when the meal was finished. "But since you have no boots, Finn, perhaps you would like to join me in the study." She smiled at me and I had that strange feeling again, not knowing whether to stay or run. "I believe you were reading a book of mine yesterday."

"Yes, ma'am."

"Tally," she said, moving down the hallway.

"Yes, ma'am."

I don't believe I ever enjoyed myself as much as I did that evening with her. As it turned out, she did private tutoring for a few of the children of the wealthy in town, making a living at it. She didn't say how she had come by the house and I didn't ask, for there are some things a man didn't do in those days, and prying into another's affairs was one of them. It was simply proper upbringing, and to do otherwise was considered pushy. And like I had told her, I didn't want to get on her bad side.

I never will figure out why when two men get together to talk it's called "stretching the blanket," but when a couple of women do the same thing it's called "chatting." I reckon you could say that we spent the first hour doing a bit of both, just getting to know each other. The rest of that evening we talked of books and took turns reading aloud from several different volumes. I'd not given it much thought before, but it crossed my mind then that what we were doing that night was one of the big differences between me and my brother Nathan. If Nathan could find someone who had an interest in guns and Rangers and could tell a tall tale, well, he was pretty satisfied. But me, I usually found myself looking for someone who'd read a book I hadn't and was willing to trade it for another. Oh, I could tell and listen to stories as well as Nathan or anyone else, but I tended to take more notice of people than Nathan did, and in a different way. I had developed the habit of placing them in one of the books I'd read to see if they'd measure up to the character as I had remembered him or her. Trouble was, I couldn't think of any one person Tally reminded me of; and what made it worse was I couldn't tell if that was bad or good.

"How long will you stay?" she asked later when we had gone out to the front porch. The sun had set and the only light came from the faraway establishments in town that would be open well into the night, and the street-light on the corner. From where we were it was mighty dim, but I noticed that it gave just the kind of highlight to her features that would make her striking even at that time of the evening. I know because I was taking every one of them in.

"Hadn't given much thought to it," I said, which was a damn lie, because between her and the books I was feeling more and more as though I had found something here that I might never come across again in my life.

"I've got a couple of weeks before I have to be in St. Louis to meet my brother and his family, but—"

"Why not stay here, then?" I felt her place a hand on mine and had the same strange feeling I'd had when I first met her. If she saw me blushing just then, she didn't say anything about it. "Please." She squeezed my hand and I felt warmness flow through me, as if she were transmitting her own warmth to me.

"Why?" I said, facing her. "Why me?"

"Because you're quite alive when you read aloud," she said with a smile that seemed appreciative as well as pleasing. "You know the feelings of those people in the stories, and I've a feeling that when they suffer you do, too. Besides, I haven't seen anyone enjoy reading those books of mine so much in some time." She squeezed my hand again, gently this time. "Won't you please stay, Finn?"

"I'll think about it."

Did you ever notice that there are times you can be talking and the conversation just sort of dries up faster than a muddy waterhole about high noon on the Fourth of July in the Panhandle? It doesn't matter what you're talking about or who with, it just sort of happens with no explaining it. Well, that's what happened then with us. And in a way I was glad, for it gave me a chance to think, and it was then that it hit me about Tally. It was then I thought I'd placed her.

"Talia." When I said it, she gave me a curious look. "That's Greek, isn't it?"

"Yes," she said, although she didn't seem surprised that I had said it. "It means 'blooming.'"

"Well, you sure are that," I said, picking the wrong time to glance at something other than her face. But she seemed to think it funny and let out a soft laugh, the kind that told you she felt little embarrassment or regret over the remark.

"Talia is also the Greek muse of comedy."

"That must be why you smile a lot," I said, not finding myself feeling as awkward as before.

That was when she caught me off guard. Now, hoss, I run a good six foot when it comes to tall, but she didn't seem to have any trouble at all reaching up and bringing my face down to hers. I never did put a time on just how long a body was supposed to kiss another, but I'll tell you this. When we parted, I knew she had enjoyed it for sure and had to admit that I wasn't in no real hurry to push her away. To this day I couldn't tell you what kind of expression I had on my face just then, but I'll never forget the smile on hers.

"Stay a while longer and you'll see me smile much more."

"I'll think about it," I said as she left for her room.

But we never did speak of it again. I reckon that kiss sort of sealed the agreement between us and that was that.

Chapter 8

The next morning she took a real personal interest in what kind of clothing I ought to wear in New Orleans, and by noon I was pretty well citified, with new boots, pants and shirts as well as a waistcoat to make it all look proper. I insisted on paying for my own clothing and got a few eyes to look like they'd be falling out any second when I brandished one of those gold pieces. I wasn't looking to draw any crowds, but I reckon some things can't be avoided.

Sam'l Dean had an urge to go back to the old ways of the frontier, so we spent that afternoon—and many another during those two weeks—scouting out game. I figured it was the least I could do in the way of paying for bed and board. The old-timer had a curious interest in me, always asking about "out there," as he called it, seemingly looking for some bit of information that might hold an answer to whatever question he had in mind. I'll confess I had no real interest in Dean myself, but he was the only link I had to finding out more about Tally, so I tended to humor him on those hunting trips.

"Is that the only name she has?" I asked the first afternoon out. "Just Talliafero?"

"Yep. Leaves a bit of mystery, don't it?" When I said nothing, he continued. "Long as I known her—and that's a year—she ain't never said where it was she come from or how she got that mansion back there. Oh, she makes a decent living with her tutoring and all, and she never turned nobody away, but folks sort of hold a grudging respect for her more'n friendship." A mischievous look came to him now. "Say, son, you shouldn't go around being nosy like that. Shows a lack of manners, you know."

I half smiled.

"Look who's talking."

The evening hours were a combination of reading and discussing the literature of the day. When it didn't rain we sometimes took walks simply to enjoy the evening air and the lazy way the hours should pass but never seemed to. The days went so fast that by the time we had finished our walking and talking it would be well past sunset. And at the end of those days, just before retiring, we would wind up on that front porch, as we had the first night, making small talk and enjoying each other's company. And a kiss before parting.

I couldn't deny that with each passing day I grew fonder of this black-haired, black-eyed beauty, and though I wouldn't admit it to anyone, I desperately hoped she felt the same toward me. Yet in the back of my mind there lingered the words of Dean on that first afternoon of hunting, the hint that she had no friends and perhaps didn't seek any either. I had never met another woman like her and wasn't sure that I wanted to. And Ellie's words kept coming to mind. From time to time she had told me—half in a teasing manner, I suspect—that someday the right woman would come along for me and that when she did I would know. The trouble was that with Tally I didn't know; I wasn't sure.

Perhaps it was the banker. If anyone could be expected to have a grudge against her, it would be him. Yet it wasn't the grudge so much as what he had said about the secret of Tally's past. In a way I was surprised that the man hadn't retaliated in some way, hadn't come storming up her steps the next day. But he hadn't, so whatever it was he had in mind, it appeared that he could bide his time and still get what he wanted.

It was the middle of the second week that I told her.

"I bought a ticket this morning," I said as we stood on the porch that night. "For one of those steamboats. I never have ridden one of them."

"You're really going to leave, then?" I thought I saw a sorrowful look on her face that matched the tone of her voice.

"Yes, Tally, I'm afraid so." I knew that telling her would be hard for both of us, but it had to be done. "Like I told you, I've got a family I've got to find a home for." I placed my hands on her shoulders and tried to look and sound as gentle as I could, not knowing if it was the right thing to do. "They're counting on me."

"But what about me, Finn? Don't I count?" All of a sudden she stopped, as if she could find no other words to say, then blurted out, "Oh, Finn, I love you so much," and threw her arms around me, burying her face in my chest. There were silent tears streaming down her cheeks now as she held me tight. When she squeezed too tightly and I let out a low groan, she jumped back immediately. "Oh, my! Did I hurt you?"

"No," I said, although I did feel some pain in my side.

"Nonsense," she said, regaining her composure as the note of command slipped back into her voice. "Come with me. I'll check your wound."

The bandage needed changing anyway, so she gathered up some medicinals and led me back to her room on the second floor, where she had a private bathing area. I pulled off my shirt and sat patiently as she changed the bandage.

"Have you ever been in love, Finn?"

"No." I felt myself being put in that awkward position again. "That is not until . . . hell, Tally, I don't know!"

"But surely you know what it is," she said, stopping for a brief moment. "I've seen your face when you've read those romantic scenes in my books. You look as if you know exactly how those people feel. Exactly."

"Maybe that's it, Tally," I said as she resumed the bandaging. "Maybe I don't *want* to fall in love."

The statement shocked her, and again she stopped what she was doing.

"But why?"

"I don't know, Tally. Maybe it's the reading. Maybe it's too many disappointments."

"Disappointments?"

"Yes," I said. "You see, when I first came west, ten years ago, I had a good share of book learning, even then. My brother kept telling me it wasn't anything like the heroics I'd read about in my books, knights in shining armor and all, but I wouldn't listen to him." I paused a moment, remembering those early years as she finished with the bandage. "I've been through a lot since then, Tally, and I'll tell you, death is still ugly. You might say Nathan was right. It was just a big disappointment for me." I stood up, ready to leave, but there was Tally before me.

"So now you think that the romance you read in those books will be just as big a disappointment." She said it more as a statement of fact than a question. And she was right, of course. But before I had a chance to answer, she had her arms around my neck, pulling me down to her and kissing me, long and hard. There were tears in her eyes when we parted and she said, "Oh, darling, I love you so. There isn't anything I would ever do to hurt you. Honestly."

That was one of the few times in my life that I was ever at a loss for words, for there was simply nothing I could say. As many words as I had come to know the meaning of, I couldn't for the life of me think of the right ones to say.

"Let me wash my hands," she said, wiping away the tears and running the back of her hand across her nose to stop the sniffling. Again I took a step to leave, but a hand on my arm stopped me. "Please don't go, Finn," she said and disappeared into the washroom.

"But why?"

"There's something I want to show you, darling," she said. "I won't be but a minute."

And show me she did. But it took more than a minute. And to tell the truth, friend, it wasn't like anything I had ever read in a book or seen in my entire life.

Chapter 9

"You got a fella to paint a picture of your house, did you?" I asked the next morning as Tally and I stepped out on the porch. We had both been in a good mood during breakfast, but now I saw a look of concern come to her face.

"I'm afraid not, darling." I could only look at her, confused, before she went on. "It's the house. It's being put up for auction."

"Auction?"

"Yes. The painting of a portrait has been traditional here for quite a number of years, I understand—when a house goes up for auction," she added by way of explanation.

"Was that what the fuss was with that banker in the cafe?" I had a feeling that the man had bided all the time he had wanted and was moving in to take over now.

"Yes. I couldn't make the payment this month, and Mr. Esquire is quite persistent about being punctual. He refused to extend me any credit and then threatened blackmail if I didn't conform to his wishes."

"Which were?" I never did like the pushy ones like that and was of a mind to make a stop at his bank after I picked up my ticket for the steamboat.

"You'll be late, Finn" was all Tally would respond with as she kissed my cheek. "Please hurry back. My students will be done by noon, and I've made a picnic lunch for us." She placed a firm hand on my arm, gently squeezing it. "We'll talk then."

I gave her a kiss in return, not feeling shy about it at all, although it certainly wasn't the thing to do in public.

I took my time walking through town to get to the ticket counter to pay for my passage. The looks I got this time were as surprising as the ones thrown my way the first day I had arrived. The surprise was likely that a backwoodsman like me could change his looks by applying a thick layer of broadcloth where the buckskins had once been. In a way, I reckon I sort of pitied these city folks for feeling like they did, for where I had come from we took it for granted that it was the man and what he said and did that made him, not the clothes he wore. Any frontiersman will tell you that it ain't the thickness or the kind of clothes you wear that keeps an arrow from killing you; it's how quick you can move and how fast you can shoot that'll save your hide. The only thing being well dressed for death did was hurry up the burying process.

The ticket to St. Louis was twenty-five dollars and the trip would take twenty days, or so I was told. I had first given some thought to buying another horse but passed it up right quick when I remembered the hard ride I had taken not too long ago. So a steamboat it was for this trip. I was confident I would get to St. Louis before Nathan and the others and still have time to spare. Besides, after what I had been through the night before, I could use the time to sort out my feelings about Tally. She was a wonderful woman, but still . . .

On the way back I tried to put her out of my mind by taking notice of the business establishments, looking in particular for the banker's name on one of the windows. People like this Esquire fella liked to advertise their importance in big capital letters, and sure enough, there his name was on a larger-than-average plate-glass window. I stopped for a moment outside the building, saw the potbellied man seated behind a huge desk. My first impulse was to go inside and pay off Tally's bill . . . and to tell him that he kept lousy company, at least, if the hawk-faced man seated across from him was any indication of who he ran with. The unshaven, hard features of his face and the callused hands told me that he was anything but an employee of a bank. But when I saw the dangerous look on Esquire's face as he noticed me outside his bank, I forgot all about it and pulled my hat down over my face and quickly moved on. The last thing I needed was a confrontation with either of those two.

Earlier in the morning there had been some dark clouds on the horizon, but Tally must have bidden them to disappear, for they were now heading for the distance as the sun broke through. It was enough to turn my thoughts to happier things, like having a picnic with Tally, just the two of us. Alone.

There's lots of things that'll sour a man on city living. For Nathan it was having all those buildings surrounding him and the way people seemed to act more like the heathens they complained about than any civilized folks. And I could see what he meant. "If you want to impress someone, son, hit 'em between the eyes with a good solid piece of oak," Pa had said once. "It works fine that way on jackasses." And as uppity as some of these folks seemed, I was beginning to think you could substitute the word "city folk" for "jackasses" in what Pa said and it wouldn't be much difference. But that wasn't what soured me on city living.

"Can you spare the price of a meal, mister?"

I had pretty near reached the far side of town when this man stepped out of a doorway just as I passed an alleyway. He looked to be going through hard times by the way of his dress, raggedy and torn as it was, so I stopped and thought a moment about taking him back to Tally's for a meal. It was the wrong time to be thinking, for I let down my guard. It is also the reason I got soured on city living my own self.

I only saw the shadows for an instant as a heavy canvas came down over me and I felt myself being dragged off down some steps into what I took as being the alleyway I had just passed. Now, I'm nothing like my brother when it comes to the way we're built. Nathan has big bones and runs a good two hundred pounds, and if it's fistfighting you're dealing in, well, he's a hard man to keep down. Me, I doubt that I weighed more than a hundred sixty coming out of a river washing. Still, the one in back of me had to be a big man, for he wrapped his arms around my chest and just picked me up to move me. But I learned a long time back that you make do with what you have in life, and if I wasn't as tough physically as my brother, I was one helluva lot faster!

The canvas had fallen only to my waist or a bit past, and the ruffian not holding me made the mistake of mumbling something, and knowing his position was all I need to know. I lashed out with my right foot, the hard toe of my boot striking what I thought to be the inside of the man's legs, somewhere in the groin area, I was hoping. But I had no time to notice, for I then threw both feet to my rear center and turned the toes out, just the opposite of what a body does riding a horse bareback. The movement had the desired effect when the toes of my boots hooked onto the backs of the legs of the attacker carrying me and of a sudden I felt us falling backwards to the ground.

The fall jarred his arms loose and I rolled to the right, lifting back the canvas as I did. That was when the second man kicked me in the stomach. I had a real strong urge right then to upchuck what was left of my breakfast, but I had to find out who these men were, for I never took a liking to being treated like trash. But it wasn't to be, for the man brought his heel down on the left side of my ribs and just above my wound. My arm had absorbed part of the blow, and I've a feeling that if it hadn't my whole side would have caved in. That was when I upchucked and near passed out.

There's times it's better to play possum than take a chance on dying where you are, so I simply lay there in the nauseous mess that had been my breakfast until one of them slowly pushed my body over on my back. I said a silent prayer then and thanked the Lord for at least that small consideration, although they were likely being cautious more than gentle. The canvas still covered my face and upper part of me, and I could only hope that one of them didn't have a pistol to shoot me with.

They rifled my pockets, eagerly taking the small sack of gold coins I carried with me. And when the other pressed against my side, the groan I let out wasn't fake at all as a very real pain shot through my side.

"Is this all you want for Mr. Esq—"

"Shut up, fool," the other said in a raspy voice. "Not quite," he said as I felt my Colt being yanked from its holster. "I always did want one of these."

Then they were gone.

It wasn't all that far back to Tally's house, but I'll tell

you, friend, I do believe that was the longest walk I ever took in my life. My ribs ached and the warm trickle down my side told me that the almost-healed wound had opened up again. And if my side wasn't actually caved in, it damn sure felt like it. I had mud and my own spillings all over my clothes and didn't even bother trying to find my hat, for it was likely more of the same. I stumbled more than walked back to the house, hearing disparaging remarks about my attire from the women I passed, and maybe even making a few of my own for all I know. I don't remember. All I do recall is climbing the porch steps and seeing Tally's horrified look as she opened the door.

"Kind of ruined the picnic," I said in a voice that must have been heard only by me. Then I sort of smiled, for I had made it back to Tally, my beautiful Tally. The last thing I heard was a shrill scream as I passed out.

"You got to stop doing this, boy," I heard Dean saying as I came to. I was in the same bed as I had been the first night and, just like my waking up the day after, I was naked as a newborn. When I squinted at Dean he said, "Carrying your dead weight is getting to be a burden on these old bones."

"Then you know just how I feel," I said, finding it hard to move my left side.

"Passing out in the library and then on the front steps," the man went on. "Why, you'd think you didn't have no manners at all!"

One thing I had found out about Sam'l Dean was that you could never tell when he was serious or trying to act the part of the town fool just so he could get away with something. So I tried smiling, although I didn't feel like doing much of anything. Not right then.

"How long have I been here?" I asked, hoping I hadn't missed the steamboat.

"Just a few hours. It's still the same day." He glanced toward one of the windows. "Mebbe late afternoon."

"Get me some clothes, will you, Sam?" I asked as I threw back some of the covers and painfully tried to move the left side of my body. It was then that Tally entered the room.

"You'll do no such thing," she said in that firm voice

of hers. I was about to tell her to mind her own business, then thought better of it when I saw the tray in her hands. "I've brought you something to eat."

Dean threw the covers back on me, then gave me a hand propping myself up against the pillow and headboard. I could see then that the bandage had been replaced and a wide swatch of cloth had been tied around my side. When Dean left, Tally set down the tray and came to my side of the bed. Taking a seat at the edge, she leaned over and kissed me, not long or hard as before, but gently this time, although it did leave a man with a longing. If you know what I mean.

"If you can stomach the soup, I'll bring up some beef for you." She said it in a playful way, and I had the feeling she was more interested in me than in the food.

I ate the soup and the beef and biscuits and coffee while I told her what had happened. I didn't mention that I'd heard one of the thieves start to say Esquire's name, for I didn't want to worry her. But somehow, I had the feeling that she knew what was going on, even if I didn't say so. It was either instinct or learning how to read another's thoughts once you've gotten used to them; I didn't know which.

"What will you do?" she asked after I'd finished.

"What any man worth his salt would do . . . get back what's mine." A hint of fear crept into her eyes as I said it, and I knew the fear was for me more than her. "Reach in that *mochila* over there," I instructed her, "and see if you can find a pistol in one of them." When she pulled back the flap on one bag and pulled out the pistol, she stood stock-still for an instant, seeing the gold coins beneath the weapon.

"Finn," she said, short of breath, "where did you get all this . . . gold."

"That's a whole 'nother canyon, Tally. Someday I'll have to take you down it."

She handed me the Colt and went back to the *mochila* and stared at the contents.

Being a two-gun man wasn't all that unusual back then. It wasn't anything like you seen later when the fancy gunfighters and outlaws took to sporting two of them at one time, but it still wasn't uncommon. Having a backup of anything made good common sense on the frontier, and a lot of us carried an extra Colt in our warbag or bedroll. It came in right handy when you were bucking the odds against the Comanch' or didn't have time to reload your first one in a pinch. Or when some son of a bitch stole your original. And, hoss, that was something none of us catered to lightly.

Tally pestered me about the gold coins, so I gave her just a hint of where I'd gotten them before falling asleep.

The first game Sam'l Dean and I had shot were deer. He had cleaned and butchered them, while I had tanned the hides and made myself a new pair of buckskins from them. It was those buckskins and moccasins I put on the next morning when I woke up. My side was stiff and ached to beat the devil, but I still had that Colt and my bowie knife, so if anything came along that I couldn't handle with my fists right then—and I didn't really feel like doing anything but recuperating—I at least had a couple of friends along to help me. And Mr. Bowie and Mr. Colt could be real persuasive at times, real persuasive.

"And what do you think you're doing!" Tally all but yelled when I entered the dining room. "You're supposed to be in bed!"

"You know, mad brings out the color in most of us," I said with a smile, "but it just kind of shows off your beauty, Tally. That it does." When the fire in her cheeks only got that much redder, I took a seat next to her and ran my rough hand over the back of hers. The mad was changing to worry now and she knew what I was about; but then, people that care for you generally do. "Hey. You ever meet my brother, you ask him if us Callahans don't run to toughness. There was some years back I got shot up by the Comanch' and they took a couple of arrows and a knife out'n me when they found me . . . and I'm still here." But her smile was still a bleak and troubled one. "There's just some things that you've got to do."

"I know," she said.

We ate in silence and I went back upstairs to get the Colt afterward. When I came back down Sam'l Dean was waiting for me at the door, dressed in the same manner he had been that first day I met him. Except that the buckskin jacket he now wore was concealing an old Paterson .36.

"Loaded for bear?" I asked, half smiling.

"Oh, no," he replied in a dead-serious manner. "Nothing that big. Jess snakes." He picked his hat up from the table next to the front door and planted it on his oversized skull. "I never did like reptiles . . . never did."

"This Tally's idea?" I asked as we left the house.

He shrugged. "Sorta."

"Sorta?"

"Put it this way, son," he said in the same serious voice. "I'm jess flat tired of carrying your dead weight around. Hell, somebody's got to take care of you."

I planned on getting to Esquire's bank about the time he opened the doors to the public, which worked out about right for the time it took us to get there. We were half a block away when I turned to tell Dean what I had planned, but couldn't see hide nor hair of him. Apparently, he had plans of his own.

When I got there I crossed the boardwalk to the blind side of the building's front, trying to look as casual as possible while I waited for the door to open. When I heard the key unlock the door, I stepped right into the frame of it and let the banker get a good look at me as he opened the door.

"Surprise," I said, knowing I'd spooked him for sure, 'cause I was looking about the same way I felt—meaner than hell. He began to turn a ghostly white in the face, and I pushed my way in, not bothering to wait to be asked. I slammed the door behind me and turned the key back to its locked position. "You and me got to talk, mister."

"But I—there must be some mistake," he stammered fearfully.

I hit him then. Hard. My left side might not have been good for much, but my right was still in operating condition. He landed on the floor with a thud, just as he had the first time I'd had a run-in with him, only this time there was a trickle of blood running down the side of his mouth.

"The mistake was yours, mister," I said as he got up. He had the look of a man who didn't know if he should be scared or angry, but of a sudden the look turned to one of confidence as I heard a step being taken toward me from the rear.

At the same time a rush of light came my way from the back of the building and I turned just in time to see Sam'l Dean position himself in the doorway, training the Paterson on a man with a gun pointed in my direction.

"Shooting him would be the biggest mistake of your life, sonny," Dean said. It didn't take much to see that he was itching for a fight and would take anyone coming his way. I knew then that Sam'l Dean hadn't tagged along to take care of me, as he had said, but simply to be there when the dance started. Some of those frontier habits are hard to get rid of, even in civilization.

"I don't work for you, old man." The gunman sounded as hard an hombre as I'd ever heard, although I couldn't see his face. "I work for Mr. Esquire."

"True enough," Dean acknowledged, "but are you willing to die for him? 'Cause I'll tell you, sonny, if you don't start acting *real* tame *real* fast, the liveliest thing about you is gonna be your guts spilling out onto that floor while you die."

The gunman let the hammer down on his pistol, and I reached out and took it from him, noting right off that it was *my* pistol he'd been holding on me. And that tore it!

Esquire had moved behind his desk now and was in the process of reaching for one of his desk drawers as my eyes met his again.

"I wouldn't do it," I said between gritted teeth. "You ain't paid for your first mistake yet." The Colt was in my right hand, and like I said, I can be fast when need be. I drove the sharp edge of the Colt's butt into the back of his hand as it rested on the desk. He let out a shriek, automatically pulling the hand back, grimacing as he did. He didn't see me toss the Colt to my left hand as I grabbed a handful of his hair and brought his face down to the desk top. When I brought it back there were tears in his eyes and blood streaming from his nose. He looked too damned scared to talk, but I was hoping he could listen, for I didn't want him to miss a word I was going to say to him.

"You may have some fancy set of rules that you live by, mister, but where I come from they're all the same and they apply to everyone. You understand that? EVERYONE!'' I still had a hold of his hair, so his nod was only a slight one. "Now, maybe you might get away with it right easy in a town like this, pilgrim, but don't you ever try it in my country. Take a man's horse, his guns or his woman and you're dead meat, mister. Now, it seems to me one of your lads took some gold coin of mine, and I'd like it back. *Now.*'' When he didn't answer, I said, "I read once that if you drive that bone in your nose back far enough into your skull, it'll kill you. You feeling curious?'' Fearfully, he shook his head, trying to get his voice back.

"No! But I don't have it!'' I cocked a warning eye toward him, and he kept on pleading. "Honest! I told the man that if he could rough you up, teach you a lesson, he could have what he found.'' If that was true I was out a couple hundred dollars, no small sum of money in those days. It was true that I had those *mochila* bags full of more gold coins, but I had plans for every cent of that money.

"Sam'l,'' I said over my shoulder, "get rid of that fella and wait for me outside. I've got something to discuss with Mr. Banker here about Tally.''

"Sonny,'' Dean said as the gunman stepped out of the shadows, and I turned to see him, recognizing him as the hawk-faced man I'd seen in the bank the day before, "if I was you, I'd stay out of my sight the rest of your natural-born life. You see, I fairly hate backshooters, and knowing you for what you are, well, I'm gonna kill you on sight the next time I see you.'' When he didn't seem to pay much attention to Dean, I threw in my two cents' worth.

"Mister, if you don't take advice from your elders, maybe you'd better listen to your betters. I can outshoot you any day of the week with any kind of weapon you choose. And the same conditions go for me as they do my friend there. Now, it's a big country out there, but I get around, so you might want to think real serious about heading for Canada, 'cause I got no love for the British except for their writings. And mister?''

"Yeah.''

"My family travels a lot, too, so if you ain't got

religion, you might want to learn some and pray they don't ever take to carrying a grudge."

He didn't say nothing, just gave Dean and me a hard look that said he'd kill us then and there if he had his guns back, and then left.

"Sam'l, this talk is private, so—"

"Not anymore, it ain't." He holstered his gun and pushed his hat back on his head. "Not if it's about Tally."

"What do you mean, not if it's—"

"You couldn't tell from looking at me, but she's my half sister. So if you don't mind, I think I'll stay."

Chapter 10

I only had his word to go on, but when he got through telling his story on the way back to the house, I had a feeling that Sam'l Dean was indeed Tally's half brother. At the moment, though, I was more interested in the truth of what Esquire had so willingly told us.

When we got to the house, Dean sort of disappeared while I washed up and sat in the back of the study that Tally used for giving lessons to the youngsters she tutored.

"I'm glad you made it back in one piece," she said, giving me a kiss on the cheek.

"We've got to talk, Tally." Maybe it was the seriousness of my voice that made her reply sound so gloomy as she said, "Yes, I suppose we must," and closed the doors to the study.

"He told you everything, didn't he?" she said, taking a look at my bruised knuckles.

"Yes, he did." I tried to say it as gently as I could, not wanting to hurt her any more than talking about what we must would. I was trying to figure out how to say it, how to start, when she rushed into my arms and began crying. I held her for what must have been a long time. When she slowly let go, a tiny handkerchief materialized in her hand and she dabbed at her red eyes, taking a seat.

"It was Hannah, my given name," she said after a short silence. "At least that's what I was told later. I doubt that I'll ever know for sure."

She was a bastard, never having known who her father was. But perhaps worse, she had never known her mother either, for the woman had died giving birth to her. Her childhood had been filled with beatings as she was passed from one family to another. But there were never any scars on her body, just the ones that are left on the mind, and they are the ones that take the longest to heal. My brother, Nathan, was proof of that.

The so-called father in the last family she stayed with was some sort of businessman who lived high off the hog and offered that way of life to Tally.

"I was so desperate that I took it, Finn," she said, a tear rolling down her cheek. "I didn't care what it was. I just had to get out of there and away from the beatings." I found myself taking her hand in mine, just as she had done that first time, hoping that I could somehow give her strength by doing it.

He was a businessman, all right, but he was crooked, too. In no time he had initiated Tally, who was fourteen and well into womanhood, into the oldest profession in the world. For two years she had catered to the best of those men who had money, but when she became pregnant, the man who had promised her so much said he would have nothing to do with her.

"I'd saved enough money by then to go out on my own, but the baby died in childbirth." She said the last in a low voice, as though it were not meant to be heard, much less acknowledged, then burst into tears again. I found myself standing again, holding in my arms a little girl who only wanted to be free from pain. "Can you ever forgive me?" she said when the tears came to an end.

Forgive her? What for? What had happened to her was long before I had met her and had nothing to do with me. Still, it was me she was telling her story to, and if there was one thing Tally, or Hannah, or whatever her real name was, needed right now it was forgiveness. I lifted her chin to face me, wiped away a stray tear from her eye.

"How could I not forgive you?" I said gently, hoping it would do the trick. It did and she kissed me, and I had the feeling that things would be all right.

"Oh, Finn, I love you. I love you so much."

Then she told me the rest of the story, the part that didn't hurt so much. She had wandered about the East Coast for some years then, doing whatever odd jobs were available. She learned to read and enjoyed it and soon found herself qualified to teach, one of the few professions open to a woman back then.

"I was just plain Hannah Smith then. And one night, at a church social, I sat in on a hand of poker for one of the more prominent men in town while I was serving refreshments and he had to answer nature's call." Here she smiled, remembering the incident. "I drew two cards and called and by the time he got back had won the hand for him." Then, spreading a hand out as though to take in the entire premises, she added, "And that is how I came by all of this." When I frowned in disbelief, she gave me a reassuring nod. "Oh, yes, I won it all. It was part of the pot the man won. All I have to do is pay taxes on it, which is what my business with Mr. Esquire was. I'm afraid I'm behind on the payments for a loan he gave me to pay the taxes."

"And that was Esquire's secret?"

"Not the loan payments, no. He would have taken those out 'in trade,' to use one of his terms," she said with disgust. "No, Finn, the secret was that he was one of those rich men I serviced so many years ago. Unfortunately, he doesn't want to forget it."

I squeezed her hand. "Don't you worry," I said. "He's in the process of losing that part of his memory right now. He'll never hurt you or threaten you again, Tally. That I can swear to." A smile and what looked like renewed hope came to her face. "But tell me," I continued. "How did the Talliafero handle come about?"

"Well, I'd read that Talleyrand, the Frenchman, was an opportunist, and since I'd taken to that way of life myself, it only seemed right to take on a name not unlike his when I moved here to New Orleans."

"And the *fero* was—"

"I learned to become proficient at a lot of card games when I was young, and faro was always my favorite, soooo—" She spread her hands as if to say that was the way it was . . . and I reckon it was. After a moment of silence she said, "I know you can't change the past, Finn, but I'm respectable now. I've got a good reputation as a private tutor and I honestly like this place. The house, the books—"

"You don't see me complaining," I said.

"—and you. Especially you, Finn." Then she was in my arms again and I was kissing her. "Won't you stay here? With me? I'd really like to share my life with you, darling." She said it in that way a woman has that makes it hard for a man to turn her down. But I did. I had to.

"I'm sorry, Tally," I said, slowly shaking my head. "But there's some other things I've got to take care of first. Like I said, it's my family."

"But what about me? Couldn't I be a part of your family? You don't understand at all!" She said it at the same time her eyes welled up with tears again. But this time she fled the room, and it made me feel sick, for I knew I had broken her heart. I just knew it.

We hardly saw each other again until the next morning, when I was to leave. The night had been a long one, for all I could think of was how much I must have hurt her and if maybe I shouldn't stay here after all. It was a hard night for making decisions. Did I stay with the woman who claimed a deep love for me? Or did I move on and finish what I had set out to do, find a new home for my family? It was enough to drive a man mad, but I made the only decision I rightfully could. I would go to my family.

"Samuel is bringing the horses around for you two," she said after we'd all suffered through a silent breakfast. "He'll ride with you down to the steamboat and bring the horses back." Then she disappeared inside for a moment, returning with a small book. "It's a present," she said, handing it to me. "A going-away present." Her eyes got watery as she looked off in the distance, and when she glanced my way again, it was with a pleading look and a tone to match. "Are you sure you won't stay?"

"I can't, Tally. Honest. If I—"

She gave me a quick kiss on the cheek, said, "Then good-bye," and was gone.

Dean brought two horses to the front and I mounted. Dean started his horse to gallop, but I let mine have its head and walk away from the house, not once looking back. We had been walking for maybe ten minutes when I remembered the book she had given me and saw that it was a volume of poems by Lord Byron. She had a love of poetry, that woman did, and perhaps this was another way of showing her love. I opened the book to the page held by the tassel in it. Underlined were the words to the poem "So We'll Go No More a Roving":

So we'll go no more a roving
　　So late into the night,
Though the heart be still as loving,
　　And the moon be still as bright.

For the sword outwears its sheath,
　　And the soul wears out the breast,
And the heart must pause to breathe,
　　And love itself have rest.

Though the night was made for loving,
　　And the day returns too soon,
Yet we'll go no more a roving
　　By the light of the moon.

Underneath it, in Tally's even, flowing handwriting, was penned, "No matter where you go, Finn, my heart will be always with you, for I love you with all my heart."

Have you ever noticed how a body can get so dead set in his ways that nothing could ever change him or his mind? And then how some little thing will happen or be said and all of a sudden he does an about-face just like a well-trained soldier marching to a drill? Well, that's just what I did, friend. Something about that poem or what she had written below it had jarred something inside me, and I had that mount of mine spun around so fast he could have given you change on a dime. Behind me I heard Dean yell something out, but all I knew right then was that I didn't want to leave Tally the way I had. It just wasn't right.

"Tally!" I yelled when I pulled up in front of the house. I slid off that horse and marched up the steps, carrying the volume of Byron.

The door opened and she came into my arms. "You came back! Oh, thank God, you came back! I just knew you would!"

"I didn't come back to stay," I said, holding her at arm's-length. I held the book up. "Nathan was right. You women will go to all sorts of trickery to get a man, especially when you find his weak spot."

"You mean I found yours," she said, half smiling but still a bit unsure as to how she should feel. After all, I had just said I hadn't returned to stay, as she wished.

"You know, Callahan," Dean said, riding up, "you're

gonna have to make up your mind. Boy, you're plum tuckering me out.''

"Yes, you did, Tally," I said, ignoring Dean. "I reckon I love you, too."

"Then do something about it, boy!" Dean yelled indignantly. "And quick, less'n you want to miss that boat."

"The man's right," I said. "Woman like you oughtn't be going around with just one name." A smile formed on her beautiful face. "Tally, I got some things to do right now, but when I send for you, I'm gonna tack Callahan on as your last name."

"Good," Dean said. "Now let's go."

"But couldn't I come with you? I have no family and—"

"Yes you do," I said, and this time it was Sam'l Dean who was doing the squirming. "He's ugly as sin and nosy as hell, Tally, but like it or not he's your brother. Listen to him. For a man who acts like his brain has gone to rot, he's got a mind like a fox."

"But—"

"He'll explain to you. Right now I've got to git."

"Finn," I heard her say as I turned to go.

"Oh, I almost forgot."

Then I took her in my arms and held her as close as I could while I kissed her. And for once Sam'l Dean kept his mouth shut.

I gave Dean some of the gold coins to help pay the back taxes on Tally's house while we waited for the passenger list to be read off for the steamboat. The boat was a big two-decker, much like the ones I'd heard about. I had never ridden one, but from what I knew they were supposed to be the fanciest, if not the latest, in transportation around the country. And I intended to enjoy my twenty-five dollars' worth getting to St. Louis. I figured it would take me about that long to heal proper anyway.

"Take care of yourself," Dean said, sticking out a paw as the captain called my name.

"I'll do that." I paused, at a loss for words. "You take care of Tally, you old geezer, and when the time's right I'll send for you—both of you."

Then I walked up the gangplank.

Chapter 11

St. Louis was one of the busiest and fastest-growing towns on the American frontier. Founded in 1763 by Pierre LaClede as a fur-trading post, it had gained its prominence when two explorers by the name of Lewis and Clark set up winter camp in the town in 1803 before starting their voyage of exploration into the newly acquired Louisiana Territory. Since the War of 1812, a never-ending flow of newcomers, mostly immigrants, had played a significant part in making St. Louis one of the largest river ports in the country. But it was the resurgence of the fur trade and the mountain men, an era that had just faded from existence, that gave St. Louis the reputation as the "gateway to Missouri and the West."

I had only been there a day or two, but it didn't take long to find out about the place once I got to talking to some of the old-timers there. It seemed like wherever you went, if you could find some fella who had been in or around town when it was built, you could get a fairly accurate description of its past, and St. Louis was no exception. I had found out an old codger who took to spending his days watching the coaches come into the station, so I joined him and got educated about the town at the same time. He had just taken off to get his noon meal when I saw one more coach pull in.

Hardly anyone else was paying any attention to the arrival of the stage, for the streets were full of men milling about, a good number of them armed. And any man walking around with a rifle and talking like he's about to get mad at someone is a real attention-getter.

"You keep an eye out, Callahan," I heard the driver say to the man sitting beside him as he pulled the stage-coach to a halt, at the same time taking note of the armed men. "Something's going on here and I ain't too awful sure we want to be any part of it." I saw Nathan unconsciously loosen the Colt in his makeshift holster. The stage I had been waiting for was in.

"All right, folks," the driver said, opening the door and standing aside to help the women out of the coach. "End of the line. Looks like we made it in one piece.

"What do you reckon the big disturbance is?" he asked, handing down my mother.

"They say there's a war on," I said, standing up from my seat in the shade. The driver gave me a look as though he had seen me before, but it was Ma I was watching. I found myself wondering what the hell Ma and Pa were doing in St. Louis. Ma made her way to me and threw her arms around me.

"Finn!" she said, burying her face in my shoulder. Then I found myself being greeted by everyone, holding on to Ma with one arm, shaking hands with Pa and feeling Nathan give me a wallop on the back that made me grunt some. When everyone got through being excited, I got introduced to Lisa Harris, another passenger, and Tom Dobie, the driver.

"Give me one of those trunks and let's get you settled in," I said. On the way to the hotel Nathan and Pa explained just why the whole family was out here.

"Ever since the panic of '37 things haven't been going all that well back East," Pa said, "so we picked up stakes and came west to join you."

". . . then this nervous little fella needed someone to get his dispatches to New Orleans, so I made a deal with him and got a riverboat ride out of it." Once we got situated in the rooms, I spent the better part of an hour bringing the family up to date on what had happened to me. I included everything from the Indian raid on our ranch and my Ranger duty to riding as an express cou-rier for the newspaper reporter. The only thing I didn't mention was the discovery of the gold coins, the potshot taken at me, the run-in I had with Garvey before leaving the battlefield, and Tally. The girl, Lisa Harris, listened with all of the fascination of an easterner who has never heard any hair-raising tales before.

"Now tell me about your own trip," I said, just as curious about them as they had been about me.

"We had quite a bit of excitement of our own," Tom Dobie said. Pa had made certain the stage driver would join us for a meal after he got his teams taken care of, and the man had done just that. He was big, about the same size as Nathan, I thought, but seemed to be easy enough to get along with. The only thing that might make a body skittish about the man if he wasn't used to it was the sawed-off shotgun he seemed to have as a constant companion. Even at the hotel dining room it wasn't far from his reach. "But first things first." He nodded toward Pa. "Mr. Callahan."

Pa stammered a bit, then cleared his throat as though readying to make an announcement. And some announcement it was.

"What do you think of having a new member in the family?"

"Your mother's with child," Lisa said excitedly. "Isn't it wonderful?"

"Sure," I said, "but how did you—"

"I'm her nurse."

"She's also the cause for excitement we had on that trip," Dobie added with a crooked smile.

As it turned out, Lisa Harris had stowed away on the stage when they left New York. There was a question as to whether she should be left at one of the way stations or permitted to go on once she was found out, but when Pa found out Ma was carrying a child (it was Lisa who had told him), he agreed to pay Dobie the woman's fare to St. Louis. She was a pretty enough young lady, and from the way she stole a glance every once in a while at Dobie, I was surprised that the driver hadn't paid her way his own self.

"But that was just the start," Dobie continued. "We weren't but a hundred miles out of New York, and one morning this fella named Kragg shows up with a handful of his henchmen." He paused, remembering the incident. "I tell you, I don't think I've ever seen such an ugly son of a . . . gun." He had to pause before letting out the last word, for a man could get right graphic about how he felt at times, and it was particularly hard to narrow down those kind of descriptions when you were around womenfolk.

"Ugly, hell," Nathan said. "That fella was downright mean."

"That does seem a better word to describe him," Pa agreed.

"How so?"

"It was daybreak when Kragg and his three men broke into the relay station, guns drawn," Pa said. "He claimed to be after Miss Harris, said he was going to take her back to New York because she had escaped jail. And perhaps he would have if he hadn't struck her. Nathan and I got into a fight with two of them, but it was Mr. Dobie and James who saved the day."

I frowned, not sure I could picture a ten-year-old as being heroic. But thinking back, I had to admit it was possible, for I had been only fourteen when I followed Nathan to Texas.

"I had got up a half hour before and was out in the barn fixing up the rigs when I heard these birds ride up," Dobie said. "Your Pa and brother were mixing it up with 'em when I pulled my shotgun on the other two. That was when one of them made a move for your mother, and the boy picked up a pistol and flat-out told the man he'd kill him if he touched her."

"Wasn't he brave?" Lisa asked, once again excited.

"Brave but foolish," Dobie said as a crestfallen look came to James's face. Up until that moment he had been enjoying the position of hero, as would anyone his age.

"We sent them packing," Pa said. "And I made sure to tell Kragg that if he bothered us again I would kill him." Pa was usually a peace-loving man, but one thing you didn't want to do was cross him when it came to his family. Like I said, us Callahans are strong on family.

"Just what was it this fella was taking you back to New York for?" I asked the girl.

"We won't talk about that right now," Ma said, a finality in her voice.

"Perhaps your mother's right, Finn," Pa added. "It's a rather delicate subject."

It was late afternoon now, and Ma and Ellie dismissed themselves to go to their rooms while Pa and Nathan decided to take a walk through town and Dobie left to attend to other matters. I finished my coffee as the girl caught up with James, who was staring out the front window, a sullen look on his face. The place was empty of customers, so it wasn't hard to hear Lisa as she spoke to the boy.

"I never did tell you how grateful I am for what you did back there at the way station." She stopped, a puzzled look coming to her face, and I wondered how awkward the two of them must have felt just then. "Look, James," she said, trying to look happy and serious at the same time, "maybe to Tom what you did was foolish, but to me . . . well, it wasn't nothing but brave. I'm glad you did what you did."

Then she planted a kiss on the boy's cheek and smiled to herself as a look of shock came over James. The expression on his face said that he didn't know whether to fight or run or what, so he simply stood there, watching in amazement as Lisa sauntered up the stairs to join the other women.

"Kind of take you by surprise, don't they?" I said, walking over to him.

"I guess." He shrugged.

"You know, James, a friend of mine once said that courage wasn't nothing more than using common sense." I wasn't about to confuse him as I had Sam'l Dean by telling him that my friend was Socrates. Right now the issue was courage, and I figured he was needing as much support as he could get. "Sounds to me like you made the right decision," I said, placing a hand on his shoulder. When he smiled back, I knew he was feeling better.

Something told me that those twenty days I had spent on the riverboat were going to be the only days of rest I would have for some time to come. Other than the time I had spent with Tally, I couldn't think of anything that had gone right since the ranch house had burned down. And it wasn't long after I had spoken to James that I was proved right as Nathan and Pa approached the front of the hotel where I'd taken a seat. Both were in a serious mood.

"We got trouble, brother," Nathan said.

"We?"

"It's Tom Dobie," Pa said. "Nathan saw Kragg with the sheriff a short time ago. He says they were taking Dobie to jail." When I was silent, he added, "I thought you might want to come along. We're on our way to see what's happened."

I had expected Nathan would jump right in on something like this, for if trouble didn't find him, he seemed to have a way of seeking it out. It kept his life from getting boring, I reckon. Me, I'd rather talk things out first. Not that I had anything against fighting, you understand; it was just that I'd had my fill for the past month or two.

"Is it any of our business?" I asked Pa calmly. But it was a question I shouldn't have asked, for he gave me one of those looks a father gives his son when he's disappointed in him and expects more of him. And that meant I was in hot water.

"You heard the man's story, Finn," Pa said sternly. "He saved our lives back there. Believe me, Finn. I owe the man more than a meal for that."

I stood up, loosened the Colt in its holster. "Then what are we waiting for?"

Tom Dobie was in anything but the best of moods when we found him at the sheriff's office. But then, no man is when he's behind bars. It seems that Kragg had arranged to have a judge handy when he had returned with the lawman to the sheriff's office. Considering his time valuable, the judge had held court right then and there and within ten minutes had convicted Dobie of attempted murder, stating that the prisoner was to be confined until he returned next time to sentence him. According to Dobie and the sheriff, this Kragg character had showed up with a U.S. Marshal's badge on, bringing charges of attempted murder against the stage driver for his actions at the way station quite a piece back. I thought I had run across my share of bad men in my time, most of them plug-ugly mean, like Kragg. But they also tended to be a little slow in their thinking, which was why they most always got caught. But I had to hand it to this Kragg: if he wasn't honest, he at least showed a bit of innovation when he stretched the truth.

"The old geezer of a judge said he figured six months

of rotting away in here would teach me a lesson to start off,'' Tom said in disgust. "But it was a frame. You can bet on that. Hell, Kragg ain't got what it takes to be any kind of lawman.''

"I've got a feeling you're right, hoss,'' I said. If what Nathan told me was true and what I had seen was any indication, I was willing to bet that Tom Dobie would be a good man to ride the river with. And in times like these, I was going to need all the good men I could find—at least for what I had in mind.

"Tell me, Sheriff,'' I said as we were about to leave. "If I can bring in this Kragg fella and prove to you he's a phony, will that let Dobie off the hook?''

"There's nothing I'd like better if I could do it,'' he replied. "Tom and I go back a long ways. Of course, there's still the judge's ruling to take care of, to be legal and all.''

The women were all gussied up in new dresses when we returned to the hotel, all expressing a desire to eat a late evening meal. It was nearing sunset, so I said I would buy them all a meal at one of the better eating establishments in town. As we headed for the restaurant, I could see that although Ma and Ellie were excited, Lisa seemed to be worried about something.

There was only one other patron in the place when we got there, and Nathan decided the man looked so lonely that he invited him to eat with us.

"Finn, meet Oliver T. Farnsworth,'' he said by way of introduction. "He's a bookseller rode with us on the stage.''

I nodded and picked up a menu but couldn't help noticing that the little man looked as if he had lost his horse and the saddle that went with it. Somehow, I had the feeling that he had as many problems as everyone else did.

When we weren't eating we were catching up on the past, telling one story after another. Pa seemed particularly proud of James and how instrumental he had been in saving Ma and Lisa Harris. At first it had surprised me to hear of such bravado, but I couldn't understand why James still seemed downcast when the episode was mentioned again, so I asked him.

"Mr. Dobie didn't think it was so great," the boy said, "just foolish but brave is what he said."

"You know, James," I said, setting down my fork, "you're damn near as tall as I am, and you'll likely measure out to about as big as your Pa."

"So?"

"Well, I remember a man telling me one time that it wasn't a man's size that mattered, but what was inside of him. That's what made him go, he said." I paused a moment, hearing Cooper Hansen saying those words to me on the battlefield of San Jacinto as he was dying. "Now, Tom Dobie's a good man, and a handy one, I'd say, but I'd wager that if you asked him, even he'd admit to doing some things that weren't exactly safe at one time or another."

"Your uncle's right, James," Pa said. "Besides, there are times when it isn't so much how a man does something as whether or not he ever made a try at it to begin with." He stopped, looked down at the table. "Does that make sense?"

"Well . . . sort of, I reckon." It was clear James still had his doubts about what was being said.

"Put it this way," Nathan said. "You remember the times I've told you about those men at the Alamo?"

"Sure, Pa."

"Well, what your grandpa's saying is that those men could have escaped from that place and snuck through the enemy lines most any time they wanted. In fact, not doing that was just flat foolish, because they were out-gunned and outmanned and they were gonna die sooner or later and they all knew it. On the other hand, it took a lot of guts to stay there and fight it out, knowing they'd never make it out alive, so I reckon old Bowie and Crockett and Travis and the rest were kind of foolish and brave at the same time, just like a lot of us are sometimes."

"You see, James," Pa said, "it doesn't really matter what Tom Dobie or anyone else thinks about what you do. As long as you know it's right. That's all that matters, son, as long as *you* know."

"Yes, sir. I think I understand."

"By the way, boys," Pa said when he was through eating, "have you two given any thought as to where we should go from here, now that you've no more ranch to go back to?'' Nathan was ten years older than me, but Pa was talking to both of us, knowing we shared things together as brothers, just as he had always taught us a family should. "This is your land, so I'll leave this decision up to you boys. I think your mother, even in her condition, would be willing to try whatever we can work out."

With as much gambling spirit as he had, I was willing to bet that Nathan, had I told him about the gold, would have staked out a place as quick as he could and headed back to Palo Alto with me to claim the gold I had buried. But there was Ma to consider. As tough as she could be, I knew that she was carrying new life in her and would be better off with the proper care for now. No, the gold would have to wait. Whatever we would do would have to be done with an eye out for the care and safety of Ma.

"I'm not sure, Pa," I said. "I've been hearing lots of people talking about this Oregon Territory and how rich the soil is. And I've heard a man can get by in Santa Fe, all the supplies and trading they do down there. But once in a while I get to thinking of what Lije Harper use to say about those Shining Mountains." I shrugged, uncertain. "Can't say as I've given it much thought."

"Well, I'm sure we can come up with something eventually," Pa said. "Right now, I think I'd like to see how the whiskey out here compares with what I'm used to. Let's escort the women back to the hotel and go have a drink, eh?"

"I'll buy you one, Pa," I said with a smile.

"I've been meaning to ask you where you came into so much money, son," Pa said, throwing a suspicious glance my way.

"A gold mine, Pa. I found me a gold mine." I said it with a smile, knowing none of them would ever believe it to be the truth, even if it was.

Chapter 12

If I ever get to the point where I'm in need of money, I do believe I could hang out a shingle and claim to be one of those seers and make a decent living at it. Either I was getting good at reading people's minds or there are some people you can—how did that fella say?—read like a book. Yeah, that's it.

Farnsworth the bookseller was the one who gave me that inspiration, for it was on the way to the saloon after dinner that he spilled his guts to us. We had escorted the women back to the hotel, and then all of us, James included, set out for the drink Pa wanted. As it turned out, I was right in thinking that the man looked like he had lost his horse and saddle, for in his own way he had. As the bookish, middle-aged man told his story, his oversized clothes and nervous attitude seemed to confirm the truth of all those rumors I had heard about traveling salesmen.

He had arrived in St. Louis to find that the war with Mexico was not yet a month old, and all of his plans for making a profit on his books had been upset. Not that I could blame him, for I hadn't seen people acting the way they were since Nathan and I had been down at the San Jacinto. Here they were, talking about war like we were going to start another revolution or something. It seemed as if everyone about had a long-waiting desire to start a war with someone and had been granted their wish. Word had it that President Polk had asked for fifty thousand volunteers when he had declared war on Mexico and, after only one month, had come up with near seventy-five thousand of them! And that kind of talk tended to purely fluster men like Farnsworth.

"It's not that I wouldn't expect these ruffians to do something like that," he said to me on our way to the saloon. "It's just that the civilized people back East are reacting the same way!" The way he said it, I could tell it was a mixture of frustration and anger that only added to his confusion about the whole matter.

"Oh?" I said more out of curiosity than interest. He may have been confused, but from that last statement, he seemed to know more about what was going on than I did, and that got my interest, for other than the courier riding I had done, I had no knowledge of any faster messenger service than the stagecoach Nathan and Farnsworth and the rest had come in on.

"Yes, indeed! You see, Mr. Callahan, when I arrived this afternoon, I received a message that I am to proceed to the Army of the Rio Grande where General Taylor and his men are located and DONATE my books to them!" He said the word as though it were an unholy or unheard-of term that he despised. "It seems as though a dozen or so New York publishers have decided to donate books to the men who are fighting this war."

"Sounds kind of patriotic to me."

"All well and good, I'm sure," the man continued, throwing his hands in the air in frustration. "But you miss the point! How do I make a living if I donate my books?" Before I could answer, a quick frown came over his face and he shivered. "Besides, if even half of what you said of how those men live is true . . . the disease and pestilence and snakes and mosquitos"—here he shuddered somewhat—"I don't believe I could stand it."

"It'll work out, Farnsworth," I said, trying to sound convincing. "It always does."

The saloon was a far cry from the makeshift affairs Nathan and I had come to know on the frontier of Texas. This one was a permanent structure, with fancy plate-glass windows, a mahogany bar, well-built and varnished tables and chairs, and even a bartender with a starched white shirt and bow tie. He was a mountain of a man who, in all likelihood, doubled as a bouncer when the need arose. That he looked out of place in his attire was obvious, yet as big as he was, I knew that few of his customers would seriously prod the man unless they desired to leave the establishment under less than welcome circumstances.

Nathan pulled a stool from the corner of the room for James, who took a seat at the end of the bar next to the door.

"Three ryes and something for the boy, if you've got it," I said when the bartender asked for our order. "What are you drinking, Farnsworth?"

"Well, uh," he stuttered. He either wasn't a drinker or had the idea that the bar wouldn't carry whatever fancy eastern drink it was he was used to. "I believe I'll have some sarsaparilla." He said it softly, acting meeker than usual, as though he feared someone might overhear him.

The barkeep eyed him suspiciously, left and returned with three shot glasses of whiskey, the requested soda and a glass of dark-colored liquid, which he set in front of James. "New stuff the drugstore's adding to their soda counter," he explained. "Call it root beer, they do." Then, nodding to James, "Free to you, lad. See what you think."

Pa seemed fascinated with the place, taking in the decor like he was. But it was the table at the rear that got his attention. Several men were playing cards at it. Pa seemed to notice them, too, for he nodded slowly, then tossed off his drink. "Boys, I haven't had a chance to play poker in some time," he said, a smile forming on his lips. "Don't wait around for me when you leave. You know how long some of these games can get."

"He's up to something," Nathan said as Pa introduced himself to the players and pulled up a chair.

I smiled, shook my head in disbelief. "Nathan, sometimes I wonder if you ain't the most suspicious man that ever lived."

"Could be," he said in a serious tone, his eyes still trained on the table, "but if I am, you just remember that it's kept me alive for a good many years now."

For a few minutes we discussed the possibilities of where we might go upon leaving St. Louis. Then I spotted a man at the far end of the bar and turned my back to him as he finished his drink and started to leave.

"Is that heavy-set fella at the end of the bar our man, Nathan?" I said. "Finish your drink and let's see if we can talk to him outside."

Nathan and I were tossing off our drinks when I heard a gravelly voice behind me. "You again—"

When I turned, I saw Kragg in back of me. He was too ugly to be anyone else. He must have just caught sight of James sitting there. After hearing the story of what James had done to him, I couldn't say I blamed the man for turning blood-red in the face and stopping dead in his tracks upon seeing the boy. All it took was a glance to know there would be trouble soon, and I could tell Nathan was balancing himself the same as me as he turned. But I think what surprised both of us was seeing Farnsworth take a stand right in front of the big braggart.

"I'm afraid you'll have to leave, sir. This boy hasn't—"

"Outta my way, runt."

I had to give Farnsworth credit, for he didn't budge an inch. Maybe he had more guts than any of us had given him credit for. He swung at Kragg, who caught his fist while he hit the smaller man a glancing blow to the face, sending him on a collision course into James and his chair.

Before Kragg saw me coming, I backhanded him with my right, a blow that threw him off balance. It gave me the edge I needed, and when I completed my turn, I hit him hard enough to send him sprawling to the floor near the door. I saw Nathan reaching for his Colt as I stepped in front of him toward Kragg.

"HOLD IT!"

The bartender's booming voice stopped all of us as I glanced at him over my shoulder. He held a pistol in his hand and the look on his face said he wouldn't mind using it.

"No fighting in here!" he said loud enough for all to hear, then glanced at Kragg and me. "I guarantee that neither of you has got enough to pay for the damages in this place, so take it outside." Then his attention went back to Nathan, who still had his fist wrapped around his Colt, giving the barman all the cause he needed to be cautious.

"Suits me," I said, and at the same time I hit Kragg in the face, knocking him through the batwing doors and out into the street. Once he was beyond those doors, I knew he didn't have a chance. The law was new to the frontier, and a man made his own most places he went; if he chose to settle his disputes with his fists rather than a gun, few lawmen would interfere with him. Twice Kragg got up and twice I battered him so badly that his face was nothing more than a pulp when he finally fell to the ground unconscious. I may not have been as thick in the chest as Nathan, but I was as tall and faster, and that made all the difference when it came to bullies like Kragg. I made my way through the small crowd of onlookers, saw Nathan looking over James, who seemed none the worse for wear. But Farnsworth was dabbing at the side of his mouth with a handkerchief, an angry look on his face.

"Looks like your friend Dobie was right, Nathan," I said. "Pure fat and sass. Only thing hard on him is his jaw," I added, rubbing my knuckles into the palm of my hand. It's times like that I keep asking myself if maybe I shouldn't have tried talking a bit harder, for I'll tell you, hoss, busting up your knuckles sure ain't the best part of winning a fight. I don't care what they tell you.

When the crowd dispersed, I bent over the body of Kragg and removed the badge that was pinned to his vest and the belt gun he carried.

"For a pilgrim, you're catching on fast, Farnsworth," I said, placing the pistol in the drummer's hand. At first I couldn't tell if the look on his face was simply one of surprise at being given the piece or one of fear for having such a dangerous weapon in his possession. "Soon as our friend here comes to, we're gonna escort him over to the sheriff's office. You think you can watch him till I get back? Right now I could use a good drink."

"Well, I guess. But what will I do when he comes to and you're not back?" he asked nervously.

"Tell him to stay put less'n he feels froggy."

"But what if he jumps?"

"Shoot the son of a bitch." I said it in a cold, hard voice, so he knew that was *exactly* what I expected him to do. "After what he pulled in there, ain't nobody'd blame you."

"Yes, sir," he said meekly.

"And Farnsworth," Nathan said just before we entered the saloon.

"Sir?"

"Thanks for stepping in. I'm obliged to you."

"Yes, sir." Somehow, hearing Nathan say that did something for the little man, and I got the feeling he wasn't as uneasy as he had been a minute earlier.

We had another drink before leaving, Nathan all the time watching Pa at the poker table.

"I still say he's up to something."

Kragg was regaining consciousness when we left, and we made him stagger every painful step of the way to the sheriff's office. I let Farnsworth tell the story as Sheriff Cameron took more than a casual interest.

"I'd say those assault charges will stick, but I doubt that you'll have to file them, Mr. Farnsworth," he said. "You see, I did some checking up of my own on Kragg here." Kragg's forehead seemed to be the only part of his face that wasn't covered to some extent with blood, and looking down at him, I could see beads of sweat begin to form. "Now, you've got to remember that Tom Dobie does some exaggerating at times. But when he told me this fella was low enough to steal that badge off a dead man, I got to thinking.

"A week ago there was a corpse of a man, a U.S. Marshal, that showed up. So I checked with Jonah, the man who does most of the undertaking in our town, and what I found out was right interesting, because I described Kragg to Jonah, and he said it fit the description." His glance shifted from Kragg to the hallway of cells as he reached for the ring of keys.

"What description?" Farnsworth asked excitedly. "You mean this man actually stole a badge from a law enforcement officer?"

Sheriff Cameron walked over to Tom Dobie's cell, inserted the key in the lock. Dobie, who had also been listening, was as confused as the rest of us.

"No, it goes a bit further than that. You see, Jonah said the man had papers identifying him as a marshal, but he didn't have a badge. He also said that Kragg was the one who brought the body in to him." He turned the key, swung the door open. "Kragg, I'm placing you under arrest for the murder of that U.S. Marshal." Then, looking at his friend, he added, "Tom, you're free to go."

Kragg said nothing, hardly made a fuss as the sheriff locked him up and Dobie gathered his belongings.

"Don't you think there's gonna be a question of guilt, Ray, when you get this fella before the judge?" Dobie asked.

The sheriff only smiled. "I doubt it. Especially after the judge finds out he's prosecuting the man that made a fool of him and put you away."

"Wait a minute," I said. "I thought he was supposed to be in some kind of hurry to be on his way."

"Oh, he is, all right," the sheriff said. "But if there's a poker game going and he can find it, old Judge Rogers ain't likely to pass it up. No, I wouldn't worry about not finding him to get Tom's papers taken care of. Especially on a Friday night."

Nathan had that I-told-you-so look on his face that went along with a wide grin as we left the sheriff's office and stood for a moment on the boardwalk.

"I told you Pa was up to something," he said with a smile.

James and Farnsworth headed back to the hotel to turn in, but Nathan and I went right back to the saloon to see just what it was that Pa did have in mind, if anything.

The game had been going for the better part of two hours by the time we were back. Maybe I'm getting old or else Pa still had better eyes than me, for it wasn't until Nathan and me edged our way down toward the end of the bar that I got a better look at the players. One in particular, a gray-haired fella who looked to be pushing sixty, seemed to be the most fired-up cardplayer. When he wasn't laying down cards, he was ranting and raving about the war and the uselessness of anyone who opposed it. I had no doubt that this was the judge Tom Dobie had described, and asking around proved it out. But Pa must have figured it out, too, for he had spent upwards of two and some hours playing a steady game with this fella. Which isn't a bad idea when you're playing cards with total strangers. You get to study them and see what they do and don't do, and that can be dangerous to them. For instance, this man tended to get real excited when he had a winning hand and just couldn't wait to throw down his cards and rake in the pot. Fact is, I was beginning to wonder if he wasn't greedy enough to maybe have taken some money on the side to get a quick conviction of Tom Dobie earlier.

Finally, one game came down to just Pa and this judge, and I knew by the look on his face that he had a good, solid hand, that he wasn't bluffing. As for Pa, well, you never could tell what he might have. Nathan and I had played some with him in our younger years, and I swear we could never tell when he was bluffing or not. And tonight was no different. I just found myself hoping he knew what he was doing with his money.

"Well, Callahan, we have been playing all night without doing much of anything. Now, I've got a good hand, and I mean to make something of it," the judge said in that confident voice. "I'll go you a hundred and fifty dollars."

"I'll see that and go you a hundred and fifty better," Pa said, glancing at his hand. Then I thought I saw a smile form at the corners of his mouth, as though he knew something no one else did. But who could tell? I had seen that same expression on his face when he had been bluffing.

The judge examined his winnings on the table, looked to be doing some figuring, and finally fished into his pocket, bringing out another handful of cash. He threw it on the table and in his determined, excited voice said, "By the Lord, Callahan, I believe I can beat you, and we'll close the thing up this time. I go you that and a hundred and fifty better."

As absorbed in the game as he was, the man could have been playing with the devil himself, and it wouldn't have mattered; he seemed that confident.

"So you've a good hand, have you, Judge?" Pa said, still smiling. "Well, I suppose so, for you don't seem to be bluffing." He was silent for a moment, glanced down at his hand, then back to the judge. The old man was overly anxious now, could hardly wait to throw his cards down and take in his pot. "But I believe I have a better hand, sir. I'll go you that hundred and fifty, *and custody of Tom Dobie*."

"Done," the judge said quickly. "I call you!"

The judge laid down an ace-high straight and began encircling the winnings with his arms, not even caring what Pa held. He was pulling the money toward him when Pa's huge fist came down before him, revealing a flush in spades. The old man looked as though he would drop dead then and there as Pa dropped his cards and pulled the scattered heap of bills and coins toward him.

"I'll see you at the sheriff's office tomorrow morning, sir?"

"Huh? Oh, yes," the judge said, still in a state of shock.

Nathan didn't have to say anything as his grin spread from ear to ear.

"I know! I know!" I said. "He was up to something."

But Nathan just smiled.

Chapter 13

The next morning we ate in the hotel dining room. When we had finished, Nathan, Pa and Dobie headed for the sheriff's office, where they were to meet Judge Rogers to legalize the release of the stage driver. James escorted Ellie to the store to pick out a new dress, and Ma and Lisa Harris returned to their room. Me, I wanted to catch up on my reading and propped a chair out in the hallway to catch the cross current of breeze that came from my own window and the one at the end of the hall. I reckon Ma and Lisa had the same idea, for their door was half-open as well. Not that I'm an eavesdropper, you understand, but with the door open like that it did make it kind of hard to not hear what they were talking about. And in a way it didn't surprise me that the subject was Tom Dobie.

"Do you love him?" I heard Ma ask.

"Me? Him? I . . . How did you know?" Lisa asked in what sounded like a surprised voice.

I knew Ma was smiling from the way she said, "It's hard not to notice. But you wouldn't know anything about that, would you?"

"But how could . . . ?" The girl still sounded as though she was a bit shocked.

"Lisa," Ma said in that motherly way she had, "ever since you've become a permanent part of this journey we're on, ever since that incident back at the way station . . . well, girl, you sit next to Tom Dobie—or across from him—whenever we eat. You pour his coffee first and last and you always make sure he has more than his fill of food. There's probably never been anyone as kind and courteous to him as you've been. And you follow him around like a pup.''

"A pup?" Lisa sounded even more confused.

"I guess that's not the right word," Ma said, and I knew she was still smiling, still enjoying it. "I suppose in a sense it would be more appropriate to say that Tom Dobie is to you what his grandfather is to James." There was a pause and I remembered how Pa and his only grandson seemed to be together nearly all of the time. "Those two have discovered a new adventure in their lives, and if they were to lose it, I don't believe they would know what to do."

"But what's that got to do with Tom and me?"

"The way you look at him, the way you act toward him," Ma was saying, "well, you may not admit it to yourself, Lisa, but I'd suspicion that Tom Dobie means just as much to you as James and Liam do to each other. Why, Lord, girl! You're courting him, whether you admit it or not!"

"I guess you're right," Lisa replied, sounding as if she was on the verge of tears, the way a woman does when she sniffles that way. "But it sure don't seem like I'm getting anywhere. He's got more interest in those horses of his than he does in me. Besides, I was taught that it wasn't ladylike to do the courtin', that it was the man who was supposed to do it."

I heard two chairs scrape the floor as Ma said, "Have a seat, Lisa." Then, after another moment of silence, she said, "It's forty years now that Liam and I have been married. We were both fourteen and you know, Lisa, sometimes I wonder how we put up with one another, as much as we've been through. But we have. I suppose it was a bit like coming to this new land, in a way. If you love it as much as my boys do, you learn from it and accept it and change with it. And I've loved Liam right from the beginning." There was a tenderness in her voice now, the kind Pa and Nathan and me had gotten used to whenever she'd talk proudly of us. "But I'll tell you something, lass. If I'd have left it up to Liam, there would never have been a marriage.

"He was so tall and strong, and I do believe he could have fought an army by himself if he had to." She laughed, softly now. "And to hear him tell James, he has! But he couldn't face a woman then, couldn't find it in him to say what he felt. So I helped him along, shall we say.

"Oh, they taught us the same as you've heard, that the man does the courting and all. And you'll hear till the day you die how it was the man married the woman." Her voice then dropped so low I could barely hear it, as though what she was about to say was part of some conspiracy. "But don't you believe it. Let the men believe it, if they like, but don't you believe it." There was a pause and an encouraging tone in her voice as she said, "If you want Tom Dobie, young lady, you get his interest in you so high he won't even notice those horses. Just help him along and show him you mean business . . . if you know what I mean."

Somehow, hearing that made me understand Tally a bit more.

I met Tom Dobie and Nathan at the sheriff's office, and we set out for the stage depot. Pa and that old judge headed off somewhere, and from the sounds of them when they left, they'd be seeing who could come up with the best story of a lively poker game.

"There's your fifty dollars, Mr. Dobie," the stage master said behind the depot counter. "The company's gonna miss a man like you, but luck to you," he added, offering a hand. Dobie took it, knowing it was offered in sincerity.

"No offense, Wally. I just never got used to being tied down to one place or one outfit all that long."

"None taken. Next time you come by, we'll have a beer."

"You bet." Nathan and I had been standing on either side of the entrance while the transaction took place and were a bit surprised when Dobie said, "Oh, you," as he turned to leave. I didn't understand it until I looked down to see Lisa Harris standing just outside the entranceway. But Tom Dobie just brushed her aside as he left and plunked himself down on a bench outside the office as he counted his money. Nathan and I followed Lisa out as she sat down next to the man, who all but ignored her.

"So you quit, huh?"

Maybe she didn't know we were there, but when I heard the tone of her voice and the look in her eyes, I got the feeling she didn't really care if the whole town heard her.

"Yup."

"Where are you gonna go?"

"Don't know," he said, looking out across the busy street. "Mountains maybe. God only knows I ain't staying in this so-called civilization any longer than I have to." Looking about him, he seemed to take in the hugeness of the buildings around him and shook his head in disgust. "Hard enough putting up with stagecoach passengers," he added. "How a man could put up with this, I'll never know."

"Tom?" She sounded cautious now, as though she were not sure what to expect from him next, her confidence gone.

"Huh?"

"I like you."

"What?" he frowned. "What did you say?"

"I said I like you." There was nothing shy about the way she said it this time, real loud and clear.

"Now, what do you want to say that for?"

"Well, a woman can say what she wants."

"Woman!" The man was plainly irritated now and said it as though she had a lot of nerve to even make such a statement. "Why, you're nothing but a kid!"

"I'm twenty-two, Tom Dobie, and—"

"And I'm twice your age, so you ain't nothing but a kid."

"Oh, hell!" It wasn't often you heard a woman go to cussing, even on the frontier, so I reckon her saying that sort of threw all of us off a mite. But I think it had the effect she wanted, for it was when Tom Dobie had that flustered look on his face that she leaned over and kissed him, real hard.

"Finn, I don't recall seeing teeth like this before, do you?" Nathan said, opening the jaws of a horse hitched next to us. When I threw him a curious frown, he said, "Believe me, little brother, I know how the man's feeling about now, and lest you've an urge to die young, I'd find a real sudden interest in this here mare's teeth." I took the hint right quick.

But like it or not, I was also standing off to the side and had a clear view of Lisa and Tom kissing each other. And I'll tell you, hoss, they sure did seem to enjoy it some. And it wasn't no little peck on the cheek they was giving out either. But when they were through, the damndest thing happened. His face still looked like the usual granite a body would think it was made of, but Lisa had a grin on her face that stretched from ear to ear.

"Damn it! What did you go and do that for?" I'd no idea what was going through his mind while they were kissing, but he was back to being irritated by her presence. Trouble was, it didn't do a lick of good, for she was still smiling at him. "People don't do that stuff in public. Why, I don't even know you. Besides, that stuff is for—"

He never finished saying it, for James's shouts from across the street interrupted him. The boy was running pell-mell straight at us, yelling all the time.

"Pa! Pa! He's got Ma! He's got her!"

Out of the corner of my eye I saw Dobie pick up his shotgun and walk over to us as James neared. But what really caught my attention was the sight at the far end of the block. It was Kragg, a pistol in one hand while he held Ellie in front of him for protection with the other. Somehow or other he must have gotten out of jail was all I could think as I pointed him out to Nathan.

"I see him," he said with that kind of slow-building mad that made him a dangerous man.

"He got out, Pa! That man," James said, out of breath and pointing, "he got out!"

"Just calm down, son," Nathan was saying as I checked the loads of my Walker Paterson. Then, turning to Dobie, he said, "That sheriff friend of yours had a couple of Patersons in his office, didn't he?"

"I think so. Why?"

"If Kragg's got one," I said, reading Nathan's mind, "he's likely feeling sporty."

It almost seemed as if all of us knew what we had to do as Nathan and I turned to go, walking down the boardwalk.

"Pa?"

Nathan stopped. "You stay put, son" was all he said

to James, and I could tell the boy was once again feeling left out.

"I'll work my way around to the street side of those horses, Nathan," Dobie said. It was the first time I had heard him call my brother by his first name. "He'll likely want to get one to get out of here."

"All right," Nathan agreed, "but no using that scattergun as long as he's got Ellie. You hear?"

"Right."

It seemed like one of the longest walks I had ever taken, and I knew it must have been longer for Nathan. Still, there had been no shooting yet, so perhaps the man was simply bluffing. I glanced over my shoulder to see if James was still there. He and Dobie were in some kind of hushed conversation, the driver probably telling him what Nathan and I had no time for right now—that this was a man's fight, and a young boy that wasn't quite between hay and grass yet would only complicate matters.

By that time we were halfway down the block. I never will know if it was looking back like that that saved me or not, for I felt my hat fly from my head before I heard the shot from Kragg's pistol. That tore it! I'd had more than my fill of being potshotted of late and was damn tired of it. But it was Nathan's strong grip on my arm that kept me from pulling my Colt then and there.

"Let her go, Kragg," he yelled out as any curious spectators disappeared.

"Not a chance! Not till I get clear of this town." He sounded desperate now. He had been waving the pistol from side to side in front of Ellie in case anyone got in his way, but of a sudden he pointed it at her temple. When he did, I felt Nathan's grip on my arm loosen altogether, knew that he had the same fear and anger running through him then that I did. "I'll kill her! I swear I will, Callahan! You just back off and let me get out of town."

"Kragg!"

The voice surprised all of us, especially Kragg, for it came from his street side, and when he looked, even at that distance, I knew he had a new fear of his own to handle. Pa stood way off to one side, a pistol extended at arm's-length and aimed directly at the outlaw. I had never heard Pa talk of dueling or gunfights of any kind, but he looked so cold, so deliberate, out there in the open that I would have sworn he had been doing it all his life. But then, Pa was like that, real good at pulling off surprises and all.

"I told you once, sir, that if you ever laid a hand on any of those women, I would kill you!"

"And?" Kragg must have known he was about to die, for he spoke in a careless manner now.

There was a long silence then as Kragg kept looking at Pa and waiting for him to make a move. And it was then that Nathan and I started walking again, right toward him, guns drawn and ready to fire. It crossed my mind that it was the likes of Kragg and his kind that I would enjoy watching die a slow death, but right then it was going to take a fast, quick shot to put him away and keep Ellie alive.

But I'll be damned if it wasn't James that started the ball! All of a sudden here he came, running out of the side alley on Kragg's blind side, tackling Ellie and falling to the ground with her. And for an instant I thought I saw him roll over atop of her so as to shield her from taking a slug.

That's when hell took a holiday.

Kragg and Pa fired at one another at the same instant and it looked like both shots hit their mark as both men staggered backwards. Pa's shot had hit Kragg in the arm, spinning him to his left so that he faced us. And friend, you never seen two brothers do anything so fast, so accurate and so right at one time. Nathan and I raised our Colts and fired, almost as one shot. Both slugs hit Kragg in the chest, sent him staggering to the rear. And if he wasn't already dead on his feet, he damn sure was when Tom Dobie stepped out from behind those skittish horses at the hitch rail and let fly with his shotgun. Kragg took both barrels in the chest, and I swear there couldn't have been more than his backbone holding him together, there was that much blood flowing out of him when he fell to the ground!

"Dumb son of a bitch," I heard Dobie say, looking down at the man. "Told him I'd overload."

The look on Nathan's face was a mixture of happiness and anger that didn't know which should come out first.

"You all right?" he asked when Ellie ran into his arms.

"My God, Nathan, I was scared!" was all she could say. "He was going to—"

"No more, honey," he said to her softly.

"That's right, Ellie," I said, looking down at the bloodied remains of the man. "This 'un ain't gonna do nothing no more."

"And just what in the hell caused you to pull such a damn fool stunt, James?" It was the anger in Nathan coming out now.

"I saved Ma's life," the boy said proudly, wiping the dust from his clothes.

"I told him to," Dobie said with the same coldness in his voice as when he had spoken to the dead man. "Look, Nathan, the only way we could get a clear shot at Kragg was to get Ellie out of the way. Now, if you, Finn or I tried that stunt, we'd have broken every bone in her body. Way I figured then, and still do, now, James was the right size for what was needed." He cocked an eye toward Nathan, as though waiting for him to challenge the logic of his statement. "And like the boy says, he did save his mother's life."

"He's right, Nathan," Ellie said, regaining her composure.

"Nathan! Finn! Quick!" Across the street, Lisa was kneeling next to Pa.

When we got to his side, he was lying on his back, a steady pool of blood forming on his shirtfront, slowly spreading. Lisa knelt next to him, silent tears rolling down her cheeks.

Nathan fiercely grabbed her wrist. "Well, do something, damn it! You're supposed to be a nurse, ain't you?"

Slowly, Pa reached for Nathan. "There's not much she can do, son," he said, grimacing. "Did I—"

"You got him, Pa," I said. "First shot. He won't threaten no one no more."

"James?" he asked, as though searching his memory. "Was that James?"

"Yes, sir, Mr. Callahan," Tom Dobie said. "It was for a fact. Saved his mother's life, he did." His words were for Pa, but there was a hard, cold glare that settled on Nathan as he said it. James saw it, too, and for the first time since the shootout, likely had the idea that his father was mad at him.

"Grandpa," he said. "Was that dumb . . . what I did? Was I foolish?"

"No," Pa said, choking. "Not foolish at all." It took all he could muster to force a smile then, but I figure he knew he was dying then, and every dying man has more things to say than he has time for. "Fact is, that's 'bout the bravest thing I've ever seen." Then he slowly closed his eyes and his head rolled to one side.

"Grandpa?" There was an urgency in the boy's voice now.

Lisa took hold of his shoulders then, the tears still in her eyes. "He's dead, James. I wish I could say something but—" She put her arms around him and held him as if he were her own kin. Then, after a few minutes of silence, she and Ellie went back to the hotel to tell Ma.

That whole business of Pa's dying like that sort of did something to me. And I reckon the same feeling came over Nathan, too. A man's life don't make an easy pillow to sleep on, and the loss of Pa and the way we would miss him would cause more than one sleepless night for Nathan and me.

I could vaguely hear someone call for an undertaker while the crowd got their look at a dead man and went on about their business. But for the most part I reckon we just stood there wondering what we'd do with Pa gone now. Oh, we were full grown and as capable as any man of living his life, but there's something about your own flesh and blood that dies in you when they pass on; something that will always tell you you never said enough or often enough what you should have. And it'll haunt you till your dying day. I don't know about Nathan, but that's what I was feeling about then. I didn't really have the urge to go on thinking that way, but I might have if I hadn't heard Dobie and Judge Rogers discussing something over on the boardwalk a short distance off.

"Just what I figured," the judge was saying as he dug something out of the woodwork of one of the storefronts.

"How's that?" Dobie said.

"Wasn't Kragg that killed Callahan," the man said, and all of a sudden I wasn't thinking about anything else.

"What do you mean?" I heard Dobie ask as I walked toward the two. "I saw him shoot at Callahan."

"Sure he did. But if you check this," he added, opening his hand to reveal a lead ball, "against Kragg's gun, I'd wager it's a thirty-six caliber."

"What are you getting at?" I asked, examining the slug.

"See that livery over there?" he asked, pointing toward a stable across and down the street some hundred yards. "Well, when the fracas started, it was my pistol Liam borrowed when he decided to take on Kragg. I ducked inside that door I just dug that lead from and took to watching this whole show."

"And?" He had my curiosity up.

"And it was Kragg's slug that hit the frame. That much I know for sure. But when you boys started firing those cannons of yours, I'd swear I saw a muzzle flash from over by that livery entrance. When I get the coroner to dig out the slug in Callahan, I'm putting my money on at least a Hawken Fifty, 'cause Bub, when that bullet hit Liam, it hit with the kind of thud you can hear, if you don't feel it."

Several men had come with a stretcher to carry Pa's body off to the funeral parlor, Nathan accompanying them.

"What say we take a walk, Finn," Dobie suggested, and I nodded my agreement.

The livery stable was larger than most liveries I was accustomed to, with a huge hay loft encircling the ground-floor entrance. It looked peaceful enough, but when we went in, it was with guns at the ready.

"Hey, don't shoot!"

A teenage boy emerged from the rear cubicle of what must have been a makeshift office.

"Ain't nobody here but me, and I've got nothing worth stealing," he said.

"How long have you been here, son?" I asked with an edge to my voice. I was in no mood for anything less than straight answers and wanted the lad to know it.

"Came back just a while ago, when the shooting started. I was out to eat and heard the gunfire and headed back, figuring someone was running off my horses."

"Was there anyone here when you got back?"

"No," the boy said quickly. "But there had been. You could smell the gunpowder all over the place."

I holstered my pistol and went out the back door to the corrals.

"Did you see him at all?" Dobie asked, following me.

"Well, sort of."

"Sort of?"

"Yeah. I didn't get a good look at the rider, but he was riding a buckskin—"

"And it had a bald spot on the rump," I said, stepping back inside.

"Yeah," the boy said enthusiastically.

"Garvey," I said, striking one fist into the palm of the other. "Damn him anyway!"

"Well, now," Dobie said with a jaundiced eye cocked toward me. "You want to tell me just what kind of a game I've dealt into?"

He sure could get high and mighty for claiming to be as free and easy as he did, and it was times like this that I didn't care much for it. So I eyeballed him just as cold and hard as he had me, so's he'd know I could be all business, too.

"If and when you ever buy into anything concerning me, Dobie, I only guarantee one thing."

"Oh?"

"You'll know exactly what it is you're getting into. Right now we're gonna check with Nathan about making arrangements with the undertaker for Pa. Then we're gonna find out just who's gonna take a hand in this game you think I'm playing."

It was late afternoon before all of the arrangements with the undertaker were completed. Judge Rogers provided a doctor to dig out the bullet that had killed Pa and proved his theory to be a correct one. The bullet was a .54 caliber and was most likely from a Hawken or one of the many heavier muskets used by the militia. But that didn't mean all that much to me, for the only thing on my mind now was the certainty of who the assailant was who had killed Pa.

It was Garvey, for sure.

That the man was following me was a certainty I couldn't avoid. But why? True, the man had tried to kill me at Palo Alto where the old man had buried the gold, but if he knew of the gold, would he not have dug it up himself and headed somewhere he was little known? More than likely it was just Gravey's way of getting revenge for showing him up the way I did, this shooting at me and mine. It was his style. He was the type who would rather shoot at your backside than face you out in the open, and the only certainty about men like him, if you could call them men, was that they never lasted long. Someone always stopped them short.

Where we would go from here was also a question that had to be dealt with. My instincts told me to head on back to Palo Alto as soon as I could and dig up whatever was left of that gold and stake a place to settle the family. But things had changed considerably since morning, and I knew that would not do. Like it or not, now that Pa was dead, Nathan and I would have to watch out for the family, or what remained of it. And right now that meant taking care of Ma, and in the condition she was in, going anyplace that didn't have medical facilities was out of the question. That meant the gold would have to wait.

I made my decision outside the funeral parlor. Judge Rogers had stuck around to check on the outcome of that theory of his, and after the arrangements had been made, we did some conversing about local news. Part of what he told me seemed like the answer to our question of where to head next, but first there were some things that needed finding out.

"Nathan," I said when he came out of the funeral parlor, "how about rounding up that drummer, getting him back to his hotel room and waiting a bit." He had taken Pa's death harder than I figured, but the suspicion in him was still alive as he frowned. "Between you and me, brother, we're gonna have us an old-fashioned war council. But if Farnsworth asks you," I said with a grin, "you tell him you've taken an interest in his books."

"That may be the only thing that'd get his attention," he said and left.

When we were in the hotel lobby, I told Dobie to let the women in on the funeral arrangements we'd made and that we'd be available in an hour or so if they cared to eat.

Entering Farnsworth's room, I had the idea that maybe Nathan just *did* tell the man he had an interest in his books, for he was a lot happier than I had seen him since he arrived. He offered his condolences and then went right back to business.

"I understand you want to purchase some of my books," he said with a smile.

"You could say that," I said. "But first things first. Nathan, I know I can trust," I said, then cast a doubtful eye on the stage driver and the salesman. "But for what I've got in mind, I could use a couple more good men. The thing is, I've got to know if you're willing to go along with what I've got in mind. Now, Dobie here thinks it's a game, so just to set you straight I'll tell you that it's a rigged one and we'll be playing against a stacked deck, and I wouldn't even take a guess at the odds of making it through alive. But if we do, I can guarantee it'll be worth it for all of us."

"And just where do you aim on going, Finn?" Nathan asked.

"Santa Fe." I studied the face of each man to gauge his reaction to the idea. "What do you think?"

"Suits me," Dobie said. "I've got nowhere else to go. And getting out of this town is one thing I'm looking forward to."

"Good. I'll count you in." My gaze fell on the drummer.

"Well . . . I don't know," the man said in a shy manner that bordered on fear. "I'm still not sure if I should follow my orders and take all of those books down to the Army of the Rio Grande. They fire you if you don't comply with their wishes, you know," he added with some concern.

"Then tell 'em to go to hell, Farnsworth!"

The little man's eyes bulged. "But I couldn't—"

"Why not, Farnsworth? I'll tell you something. You could be a good man out here. It took a lot of guts to step in between a man like Kragg and James, and you already know how grateful Nathan is for that. That's a sign you could be your own man. Besides, you don't want to go down to Texas and Taylor's army. I just come from there, and the stories I was telling the other night were only half of what I've seen." I paused a moment, remembering Nathan's mentioning that the man had an express and distinct fear of the wildlife of that area. "No siree, Farnsworth, you don't want to go to Texas."

"But my books, my job! What about—" The man was in pure frustration at the whole situation and threw his hands in the air.

"They got mosquitoes down there in Texas, Farnsworth, that can stand flat-footed and rape a turkey." I could see Nathan and Tom Dobie doing their best to keep a straight face, but one way or another, I was going to deal the drummer into this hand, whether he liked it or not. "And the rats," I continued, "well, they're so big that if you could find a pail to put your garbage in, they wouldn't tip it over to get the garbage. No, sir. They're so big they just take the pail and all."

Farnsworth quickly loosened his shirt at the collar, turning a light shade of green at the gills.

"No, Mr. Callahan," he said shortly, "I don't believe I'd like your Texas much. But what about the books?"

"Let's take a look at 'em."

Dobie set the trunk full of books on the floor between us while Farnsworth fished in his pocket for the key to it. Opening it, I saw two rows of neatly packed books, side by side, one row atop the other.

"Fine," I said. "Now take 'em out." When Farnsworth frowned, I added, "I want to see the full selection."

It was hard not to notice the titles of Milton, Dickens, Byron and other well-known authors as he removed the books. Some I had read; others I had made a note to read. But that wasn't the main concern I had as the bookseller stacked the books in two neat rows on the floor. When the trunk was empty, I stuck a fist inside and knocked on the bottom. "Just what I thought," I said with a smile, sure that I had found what I wanted. I dug my fingers into a corner and removed the false bottom of the trunk, to reveal an empty space with nothing but a small purse in the corner.

"Mr. Callahan! If it's my money you want—"

"Not hardly," I said. "What I want in here, Farnsworth, is the space. See, you don't know it, but this is a valuable trunk you've got here."

"Sir?"

"Well, now, Farnsworth, the way I see it, we've all got a stake in this trunk, a fighting one at that." I smiled, glancing at each of them as I spoke. "You see, I'd fight for this trunk if it had one book or a hundred in it, because I put a lot of value on my literature. And you'd fight for that little purse of coins in there, friend, because I imagine it's all you've got in the world. And Dobie would stop anyone from taking it, because all those years with the stage lines just soured him on thieves."

"And why else, Mr. Callahan, would this trunk be worth fighting over?"

"In a minute," I said and left the room. When I returned I had a whiskey bottle and three shot glasses in one hand, a pair of saddlebags and a shot pouch draped over the other. "This is why," I said, dropping the saddlebags in the middle of the floor with a thud. "You see, friends, when I told Pa the other night that I'd struck a gold mine, I wasn't joshing him." I set down the bottle and glasses, reached inside the saddlebag and produced a handful of gold coins.

"Judas Priest!" Dobie exclaimed. "Where the hell did you get those?"

When Nathan and the drummer expressed equal surprise, I dropped the coins, grabbed the whiskey bottle and poured three glasses of the liquid, passing two to Nathan and Dobie, keeping the last one for myself.

"This probably won't match any of those fancy books of yours, Farnsworth," I said, "but what I'm gonna tell you is the damndest experience I've ever had."

And this time I didn't leave out anything. Not the gold, the old man—or Garvey. Except for Tally . . . there are some things a man has to keep to himself.

Chapter 14

If I hadn't shown them the coins, I don't think Farnsworth or Dobie would have believed my story. Nathan would have, because for the ten years we had been on the Texas frontier, we had been getting into trouble of one sort or another. And at times it seemed like we were fated to such things, but one thing neither of us would ever deny . . . those scrapes sure did seem to liven up the lives we led as just-getting-started ranchers. That they did. So it wasn't a surprise to see the half-serious, half-mischievous look on Nathan's face when I got through with the story.

Farnsworth seemed inclined to dismiss it as mythical and said as much.

"What I want to know is what this has to do with Santa Fe."

So I explained what already seemed evident to me: that I would be more than happy to ride on back to Palo Alto to retrieve our treasure but that there would be a pregnant woman making the journey with us now. "And you can bet she ain't going unless she's got doctor's care all the way."

"And I suppose the trail to Santa Fe isn't as long or as hard."

"It's just as hard, friend," Dobie said. "I've been down it a time or two, and it's no Sunday church social. Now that you bring it up," he added, throwing a curious glance my way, "just why are we going down the Santa Fe Trail?"

"We're going with the army."

"The army!" Dobie nearly shouted. "You can't be

serious! Why, I've seen more movement in a bunch of fat old squaws than I'll ever see in any army!''

"Not this one," I said. "At least if what I hear is for sure. I was talking to Judge Rogers this afternoon after we made the arrangements at the funeral parlor, and he said now that this war is official, the president's asking for volunteers to fight it. Fifty thousand, I think he said. A fella named Kearney has been put in charge of what they're calling the Army of the West. At least they have doctors, so I figure if we can have Lisa pick up whatever she's gonna need for Ma, we've got an ace in the hole if trouble comes." And in the back of my mind I knew it would.

"According to the judge," I continued, "the best of them is some eight hundred volunteers calling themselves the First Missouri Mounted. Got a fella named Doniphan in charge of them. If he's anything like the judge's description, we'll get along fine."

"You don't figure on me volunteering for some kind of soldier duty in this outfit, Callahan, do you?" Dobie was getting a bit hot under the collar now, and I couldn't blame him. Things could be rough enough for a man when he did his own volunteering, but when someone else just threw his name in the hat without even telling him, it wasn't likely to sit right. Not at all.

"No," I said. "But as good as Nathan says you are with horses and the reins, you'd probably fit right in with the drivers this Doniphan is needing. I understand he's taking horses, cattle, wagons and most of creation with him on this journey."

That knowledge seemed to brighten his attitude some, for he would at least be working with what he knew and did best, and that'll usually make the hardest of it a mite easier for most men.

"Well, that's different," he said, smiling again. "Now, if I can find a decent assistant to work with, I might even convince myself I could enjoy going along with this army business."

"Told you I'd take care of you," I said, knowing that what I was about to tell him would give him as sour a stomach as that newspaperman I'd met had. "I fixed you right up. Yup, I surely did."

"Oh?" Dobie must have seen the look on my face, for

he was all of a sudden cautious again. "Got any experience, has he?"

"I reckon you could say he's sort of rough on the edges," I said. Something in me couldn't keep me from grinning as I glanced over at Farnsworth, whose jaw then dropped open about halfway to his chest.

"Farnsworth?" Dobie said. I'd seen men who got kicked in their elsewheres that looked healthier than the stage driver at that moment.

I nodded, still grinning, noticing that Nathan was enjoying this whole affair, too.

"No," Dobie said in pure desperation. "Don't do that to me, Callahan. Not him."

I nodded again. "He's all yours."

And on hearing that, Oliver T. Farnsworth fainted.

None of the women felt up to eating that night after the day's events, so it was only the four of us and James who ate in the dining room at supper. For the most part we ate in silence, with Tom Dobie wearing a permanent scowl that was occasionally cast at a fearful Farnsworth, who only seemed capable of returning a timid smile. There was only one conversation that took place, and it was sort of one-sided. But it was one that surprised the pure hell out of me. Nathan had never been shy about criticizing anyone in public, and for as long as I had known him, I was hard put to remember ever hearing him admit to being wrong to anything, even when he was, and surely not in my presence. It was a part of his character that I had come to accept, the fact that Nathan would rather die than admit to a mistake. I reckon that's why the conversation that night surprised me.

"Son," he said in a low voice that could only be heard at our table.

"Yes, Pa." James's voice wasn't much louder. In a way it was to be expected, for the boy had been feeling badly all day about what had happened and had barely touched his food.

"About this morning," Nathan said, clearing his throat. There was a moment of silence as he looked out across the room like a man who is looking for strength in something he sees in the far distance. It was then that it crossed my mind that Nathan was doing something that would be harder than fighting any Comanche he had ever faced. "I never laid claim to having the brains in our family, just providing for and protecting it. There's times," he continued, the words coming out slowly now, as though it was taking everything within him to push them out, "a man don't think before he says what he does. Sometimes that ain't right. I didn't think about it much till just now, but I'd have done the same thing in your place, the way I feel about your grandma and all. So what I said this morning . . ."

"You was looking out for me, Pa," James cut in. "You said it's what a father does till his boy's grown-up."

"Then I reckon you did some growing today," Nathan said and, as though the conversation had never taken place, went back to cutting up the beefsteak before him.

I knew I would never tell him, but I had a feeling just then that Nathan had done some growing that day, too.

Chapter 15

Ma took her breakfast in her room the next morning, not wanting to appear in public until the funeral. Ellie and Nathan stayed with her during that time, which left me and James to dine with Farnsworth, Tom Dobie and the girl, Lisa. We ate in silence, but something seemed strange, at least on the part of Tom Dobie, who had acted civil even toward Farnsworth when we met in the dining room. In the short time I had known him, I had come to view the man as one who was so preoccupied with his horses and teams that he cared little for conversation with anyone. Not that there weren't such men out here, as well as back East, for there were; men who became so embroiled in their work that they all but ignored the rest of the world when they were around civilization. And I had taken Tom Dobie to be one such man. Yet who could tell? The man had no visible job now, so perhaps he had decided to take it easy and enjoy his idle time.

But I put that out of my mind when I saw some of the moon-eyed looks Lisa was throwing at the driver across the table. It reminded me of Ellie when she had that way about her that told anyone who cared to notice that she had set her cap for Nathan . . . even *after* they were married. And it was times like that I found an excuse for doing other things, usually work that was far away, for a man and woman need time together. Still, Dobie knew as well as I that we had a long, hard journey ahead of us and that there would be little place for any such frivolity along the way. I made a mental note to speak to him about it later on.

After breakfast, Tom Dobie took a seat in front of the hotel, while I sat indoors, reading one of the month-old papers I had found. It was a fresh, clear morning, so the proprietor had left the front doors open and I couldn't help but hear the conversation as Lisa came from the back kitchen with a hot cup of coffee, carrying it through the doors to Dobie.

"Here," she said, "I thought you'd enjoy it." The sound of her voice with that lilt to it matched the look on her face as she passed me by, and I knew she was happy. It crossed my mind then that until I met Tally, I never really had that much luck with women, or maybe it was just that there was a scarcity out our way, but someday I would have Tally out here with me, and it wouldn't matter how scarce women were, for I wanted only her.

"Thanks," Dobie said, and I knew that in his own way, something had happened to him, too, for the voice was not the gruff one I had become accustomed to. Instead, there was almost a gentleness about it.

They were quiet for some time, and I went back to reading my paper until James came down from the room and walked past me, stopping just outside the door. And I got interrupted again.

"Is that how you spend your time, young man?" Lisa asked in what sounded like a less than pleasant voice. "Snooping on other people?"

"No, ma'am," James said defensively. "I just come out here and you were . . . there." I had the feeling the boy had walked into something he maybe shouldn't have.

"Why don't you calm down?" I heard Dobie say in an easy voice. Apparently, the appearance of the boy hadn't spoiled his mood as much as it had hers.

"Besides," James added, "I seen you doing it last night." I had to smile to myself on hearing that, for it was surely the Nathan in him coming out, straightforward and blunt. And by the silence that followed, I'd guess the boy had inadvertently caught them off guard.

"You care to jaw on that a bit more, son?" I heard Dobie ask, and I knew I was right. He was trying to act as calm and polite as he could, but you could tell by his voice that he likely had a churn rousting about in his stomach just upsetting the hell out of it.

"Well, I couldn't sleep last night," James said, "so I took a walk and did some thinking."

"And just where did your walk take you, young man?"

"Not far, Lisa. Honest! I just went down to the corner block and back. That was when I saw you and Tom."

Whether they meant for it to be heard or not, there was an audible sigh from both of them, and I found myself getting a bit more interested in the conversation outside than I did about month-old news of the war.

"You were coming back from the livery down the street. She had hold of your arm, skipping along like some kid," James continued in a tone that said he wasn't quite sure he was seeing what he was seeing. "And every once in a while you'd stop and . . . kiss," he added, and I laughed to myself, for I knew he had a look of anguish on his face to match what he said. There was another moment of silence before he said, "Mr. Dobie?"

"Yeah."

"What was Lisa doing with you in the livery?"

"Oh, well . . . I reckon she was just telling me about her childhood days and how she liked to play around in her uncle's barn."

"That's a lie, Tom Dobie," the woman said, taken aback. "I was helping him pitch the hay from the loft," she said to James, trying to sound as honest as possible.

My curiosity was getting the better part of me, and I set the paper aside and stood up next to the doorway. But the three of them were so taken up with their conversation that none of them saw me.

"Don't you believe her, son," Tom said. There was a twinkle in his eye and a hint of mischief in the voice as he turned to Lisa and said, "If anyone did any work last night, it was me."

"Well, I never!" she said in a huff, this time looking genuinely upset.

"I wouldn't say just that," Dobie added with a smile, all the time watching as her eyes got bigger, then she arose and stomped off loudly back into the hotel, giving me a dirty look as she passed.

"That oughtta wake up the guests," I said with as straight a face as I could manage.

"Does she like you?" James asked, oblivious of my presence.

"Well, I reckon," the driver said, throwing a cautious glance my way. I had the feeling he wasn't too keen on letting me in on the goings-on of his personal life. Then he turned back to James and chuckled. "Women these days remind me of that clumsy excuse for an army this nation's got."

"Sir?"

"You can't live with 'em and you can't live without 'em. Or so I've been told." As he said this last, he raised an eyebrow in my direction.

"I ain't never gonna get married!" The boy said it with the same defiance I imagined he must have used in standing up to Kragg.

"Oh? And what brought that subject up?"

"Well, I just figured that if she likes you, you like her back," the boy said, trying to sound grown-up. "Besides, I never seen anyone stutter and stammer as much as you did last night coming back from the livery with Lisa. Except for my Pa when he's bringing Ma back from a dance. He says he gets tangle-foot of the tongue, whatever that is."

"I think I know what he means," Tom said slowly. He was silent for a moment before turning back to James. "Look, pard, how about doing me a favor?"

"Sure, Tom," the boy said, his eyes lighting up.

"Let's keep this conversation under our hats, all right? Just between us men." I thought I caught a side glance in my direction as he said it.

"Sure," James said. The boy was delighted to be called a man. "But can you do me a favor, too?"

"I can try."

"Tell Lisa to stop kissing me. I don't like that much."

"Right," Tom said, a smile forming on his face. "Us menfolk have got to stick together."

"Yeah," James said. Then he was gone.

"Don't look at me," I said when Dobie gave me another sidelong glance, as though to find out what I had in mind. "I'm all against marriage, too." I knew good and well how I felt about Tally and what I intended to do, but like I said, there are some things a man's got to keep to himself. I turned to go inside and finish my paper, stopped and looked back at Dobie. "Say, Tom?"

"Yeah?"

"Are you sure it was just hay you were pitching last night?"

The back of his neck started to turn a crimson red as he slowly rose, placing his hat forward on his head.

"That reminds me," he said. "Some of those horses must be *awful* hungry by now."

We buried Pa in the town cemetery. The undertaker had originally planned on a funeral in potter's field at the other end of town, but when I gave him an extra ten dollars, the man suddenly changed his mind. When the man asked specifically why I wanted Pa buried in the town cemetery when we'd be heading west and likely never see the gravesite again, I just said, "It's something I want for my pa."

When it came time for the burial, Nathan carried the small family Bible with him to the cemetery, it being expected that, as the oldest son, he would give the eulogy. But when he saw the curiosity seekers who attend such occasions only because they are inquisitive as to what is going on, he handed me the book, saying, "You're better with words than me."

"I was never good at this," I said, taking the book as I began to speak. "In a way, I'm thankful for that.

"There's not much to say about my father. Liam Callahan was a good, hard-working, honest man, like most of the people he knew. He was a man who loved his God, his family and his country, although there were times he juggled those priorities around some. If he was rich, it was in having a family that returned that love. And I suppose that if I'm making him sound like some-one special . . . well, it's because he was my father." I paused a moment, trying to gather what thoughts I could. I looked at the Bible in my hand, then at the undertaker standing there in such a nonchalant manner, looking as if he were impatiently wishing the whole service was over. Suddenly, I found myself very mad at the pious-looking man in the black suit, and when I spoke next, it was to him.

"Mr. Gadney, I understand you had a question as to

why my brother and I wanted our father buried here rather than in potter's field."

"Well, sir," the man said, slightly embarrassed. "We usually bury the nameless and penniless in potter's field. Your father, I'm sure you'll admit, was just another Irish immigrant—"

"Mr. Gadney," I said between gritted teeth, "I'd be right careful what you say about my pa." At that moment I was glad I had the Bible in my right hand, for I was gripping it tightly, knowing full well that if it were not in my hand, I would likely be reaching for my Colt. "I've got more patience than my brother, but I'll tell you right off, I don't think I'd blame him a bit if he was to commence to taking you apart right here and now." The undertaker was starting to turn a purple shade at the gills, and when I looked to where his eyes were staring, I saw why. What he was staring at was Nathan sitting there a-picking at his nails with that big bowie knife of his.

"As for being 'just another Irish immigrant,' well, friend, my pa hated that term, and so do I." I held up the Bible in my hand. "As I recall, somewhere in here—in Matthew, I believe—they mention potter's field as being a burial place for foreigners. Well, Gadney, my father fought with Andy Jackson at Horseshoe Bend in 1814, and the general didn't raise no ruckus about where he was from then. So far as I'm concerned, when a man goes to fighting for his country, he kind of leaves that foreigner label behind him."

Then, without so much as an "Amen," I slapped on my hat and walked away. And I kept walking until I found me a stone mason willing to make a gravestone for Pa's grave.

I spent a good deal of the rest of the day avoiding people, and I've an idea they did the same with me, for we both of us knew that we'd be bad medicine for one another. The whole thing was eating away at me, and late that afternoon I just figured that if I was going to be bad medicine for anyone it ought to be that undertaker.

"Just wanted to let you know," I said, surprising him as I entered his funeral parlor.

"Oh?" The man was still acting as haughty as ever.

"Yeah. I'm having a stone put up as marker for my

pa's grave. I doubt that people like you will like it, but it's gonna stay there. At least, it'd better be there when I come back next year." When the tall, thin man looked at me a bit confused, I continued. "That's right, Gadney, I'm coming back. Every year. Just to see if my pa's marker is still there."

"And if it isn't?" The man said it in an insulting manner, as though he were dealing with some lowlife he was too good to speak to. Well, hoss, that tore it! I never could stand uppity people like that, so that's when I grabbed the lapels on his jacket and pulled him to within hearing distance just in case he was stone deaf as well as dumb.

"Then, you bigoted son of a bitch, I won't need my brother to tear you and your place apart." I don't recall just what my face said, but it must have done the trick, for I was feeling a strong urge to kill him right then and there. "I'm gonna do it all by myself. Piece by piece."

There's one thing I'll guarantee you, friend, and that is that when I left that death emporium, Jim Bowie and his knife couldn't have done nothing more to turn that fella sheet white than what I'd said!

Most all of us passed by the gravestone one last time before leaving. It had Pa's name, dates of birth and death and an inscription. It read "Born Irish. Lived, fought and died an American."

Chapter 16

The fella we were going to be tagging along with to Santa Fe carried the name of Alexander Doniphan, and if he had one thing, it was a reputation. A body will hear things just loafing around as I had waiting for Nathan and the family to arrive, and even before Judge Rogers told me about him, I was hearing bits and pieces about the man.

To hear them talk, this Doniphan was what you'd call a self-styled "ring-tailed roarer." He was supposed to be a giant of a man, if what they said was true, but you learn to discount such admirations when people make a man bigger-than-life in their storytelling. Still, if what I'd heard was correct, this man had stood back to back with some rail splitter back in Illinois, some lawyer name of Abraham Something-or-other, and measured out at six foot five, and that was big! Nathan and me never had measured ourselves but figured we ran close to six foot or more and that was a fair piece of man on the frontier, for your average man wasn't but five nine or five ten. Which is taking nothing away from those men, for many of them were tougher than the big ones. But that's going down a whole other canyon.

Doniphan was said to have a weight and frame to match his height, along with fiery red hair that when described to me could only remind me of Andy Jackson's. I never met the man personal, you understand, but Sam Houston was pretty good friends with him, and to hear him tell, Jackson's red hair shot straight back like bristled porcupine.

But that wasn't what impressed me about Doniphan.

According to the judge, the man held no belief in discipline, formality or dress. He was known to pitch his own camp and cook his own meals, and his men did likewise. I'd met some of those young West Point lieutenants down in Zach Taylor's army, and they didn't impress me at all. They figured themselves the elite of the officer corps and looked down on men like Jack Hays and Sam Walker because they didn't have some fancy uniform on so's they'd be fit to bury when they got killed in battle. It was the young, inexperienced ones like them who would have nothing to do with Doniphan and his men. And that was just the kind of man I could appreciate riding the river with. Any outfit that claimed, as the First Missouri Mounted did, that each of its members could ride like a Comanche, shoot like a mountain man and fight as long and hard as any gamecock was fine with me. But none of them was as game as this Doniphan, for word had it that once he had been elected the unit commander, he let it be known around his camp that he feared neither the devil nor the God that made him, and would fight either. And, hoss, any man that can say that either has an awful lot of guts or an awful lot of bluff, and there are times it's not bad to have a good deal of both.

I had ridden ahead of the wagon when we spotted the camp. Judge Rogers had said there were a good eight hundred volunteers and more coming every day. And what I saw nearing that outfit made me believe that most of what I had heard was true. They were as ragtag as I'd heard and some more than that. No one wore a uniform, which is what I'd expected, but the clothing on the men ranged from buckskin and bearskins to city pants and stovepipe hats. It wasn't much different from San Jacinto or, for that matter, the way Cooper Hansen had described Washington's ragtag army at Valley Forge.

But even their outlandish clothing wasn't enough to keep my attention from the fracas that was brewing amongst a half-dozen of them. It was a free-for-all that those men were having at, a huge circle of volunteers encasing them. And that was when I first met Doniphan.

There might have been some in his bunch that came close to being his height and build, but none was stronger or meaner. For this monster of a man lit into all six men, cussing up a storm and throwing one after another out of the pile, using only one hand at a time. And I do believe that if he'd happened to gather up two men at once, he'd have bashed their heads in; he was that strong. Well, seeing this man throwing bodies one way and another was enough to convince me that most of what I'd heard of this Doniphan was likely true.

Like the others watching this fandango, I didn't notice the Conestoga as it approached with Ma sitting up front. It was almost laughable, the way Farnsworth was trying to manage the team, but he finally brought it to a halt as Doniphan was tearing the last of the combatants apart, still swearing a blue streak.

"Sir!" It was Farnsworth's high, squeaky voice that caught the big man's attention now.

"What?" There seemed to be a reservation in Doniphan's own voice as he viewed Farnsworth, not sure how to take him.

"Please refrain from that foul language when there are ladies present." I shook my head, for the damn fool was at it again, trying to be chivalrous.

"Well, now, hoss," Doniphan said, smiling and slowly scratching his head. "I reckon to an easterner like you this is swearing. Yup, I reckon it sounds like that. But you see, friend, you're in Missouri now, and out here we just call 'em strong expressions."

Farnsworth was at a loss for words as he turned an embarrassed shade of red.

"And who am I speaking to?" It was Ma spoke up next, in that strong, no-nonsense voice she had. I swear there were times I think she could make Methuselah think he was a youngster with that tone of voice. And she wasn't doing too bad right now, either.

"Doniphan, ma'am. Alexander William Doniphan. I'm in charge of this outfit. And you are?"

"Margaret Callahan. These are my sons, Nathan and Finn, and my nurse and two friends," she added, introducing Tom Dobie and Farnsworth.

"My pleasure, ma'am," Doniphan said, nodding.

"I am given to understand that you are to be accompanying an army on its way to Santa Fe, and that you have a doctor traveling with you." She glanced down at the slight bulge that had begun to show in her stomach.

"We are on our way to Santa Fe, and my sons thought it best if there were a doctor near at hand."

"Yes, ma'am, Mrs. Callahan, we do have a doctor. But—"

"I'll not be a burden to you or your men, Mr. Doniphan. In fact, I believe you'll find the men in our group will be of great assistance to you in your mission. My boys are hard workers, and Mr. Dobie here knows more about driving wagons and animals than anyone I've ever met."

Doniphan smiled, glancing at Farnsworth. "And I suppose he's your assistant animal handler."

"He will be by the time I get through with him," Dobie said, casting a hard glance at the drummer.

"What about the women?" one of the ruffians sneered.

"They're spoken for," Nathan said, loud and clear. "I don't figure on fighting anything but Mexicans and Indians on this trek," he said to Doniphan, adding, "unless, of course, your boys forget their manners."

"They're playful," the red-haired man replied, half smiling, "but they'll give you no trouble."

"Then may I assume that we are welcome in your camp?" Ma asked in that formal way she had.

"Certainly, ma'am," Doniphan said.

I never did find out for sure, but I had a feeling that that afternoon Doniphan put out the word that the Callahans, and particularly the women, were to be left alone, for we never had any trouble with them thereafter.

It only took Doniphan a few more days to get his unit up to what he figured a good fighting strength of 856 men. But while more men were coming in, he was sending out those he had a company or two at a time each day. So by the time the whole outfit picked up and left, it was stretched out over a goodly number of miles in the territory and would remain that way for a large portion of the trip.

Tom Dobie took to being what you'd call a stern taskmaster when it came to teaching Farnsworth to be an able assistant, but I saw little of them. Ten years of working Texas mavericks had made Nathan and me first-rate brush-busters, and just to be doing something, we agreed to take charge of the eight hundred and some cattle that were accompanying Doniphan and his men. They were to serve as extra food and clothing in case the men assigned to hunt for the regiment couldn't come up with the required amount of meat on a daily basis. But the cattle, I learned, would go only as far as Bent's Fort and would be left there when we moved on.

"What do you think, Nathan?" I asked one day at noon camp.

" 'Bout what?"

"Pushing cattle like this. I don't ever recall anything as big as this being done back home."

"What're you getting at?" he asked, biting off a piece of jerked beef.

I shrugged. "I was just thinking there might be a market for something like this. You know, round up as many as you can and drive 'em to somewhere for a price."

"You're a dreamer, Finn," my brother said with a grin. "Hell, time you got enough mavericks together to drive anyplace, you'd waste most of the year a-doing it. Besides, St. Louis is the only big town out here, and by the time you got them cattle to St. Louie, why, shoot, they'd be so thin you couldn't sell 'em but for jerked beef," he said, holding up the piece of meat in his hand. "Never happen, Finn. They's too many easterners that are scared like Farnsworth, afraid of Indians and surviving and being their own man, to ever move out here. Let's git back to them cows," he said, taking in the last of his beef. When we'd saddled up, he looked at me and smiled briefly. "You know, brother, you're a real dreamer. But I'll give you credit, Finn. They sure are some nice ones."

It took four weeks to cover the five hundred and some miles from Independence to Bent's Fort. Judge Rogers had said that neither Kearney, who headed the regular army of this expedition, nor Doniphan was a straggler, and it was during that four weeks I found out he was right. Any other group our size might have been content to make ten, perhaps fifteen, miles a day, but not Doniphan. Kearney had his men pushing twenty miles a day, and that drove Doniphan to push his own men twenty-five and even thirty miles a day, if for no other reason than to show the high-and-mighty West Pointers of the regular army just how tough his backwoods boys really were. And that they were.

"That's it, all right," Tom Dobie said one day as we sat atop a rise. "Couldn't mistake that place if I wanted to."

We had ridden ahead that day on the scout, discovering what appeared to be old Bent's Fort at noon. I could tell by the look on his face that Dobie was certain of his find, for it was a mischievous smile that came to his face, the kind that brings back fond old memories. And Dobie had said he was once a trapper, so there was no reason to doubt him.

Even looking down on it, it seemed like the most massive work of construction I had ever seen. The thick rectangular walls measured 100 by 150 feet. Two of the walls were two stories high and enclosed a huge central patio beyond which lay an equally large walled corral.

"Looks like quite a place," I said.

"Oh, it is that," Dobie replied, that mischievous look still in his eye.

"What's so special about it?" I said, trying to jar his memory.

"Well, I reckon you'd call it a trading post. But you won't see much like it out here, Finn. Why, they got warehouses and a smithy, and a wagon shop and storerooms—" He paused for a moment, made a curious face as though remembering something of importance he had long since forgotten. When he spoke again, it was in almost a hushed whisper. "They got these . . . dormitories, they call 'em, Finn. I mean they are the damnedest things you ever saw! And a billiard table and an ice house," he concluded, a new excitement in his voice. His smile even broadened some. "I tell you, Finn, it's like seeing the circus, elephant and all, first time over again."

"Sounds interesting," I said. "If it's half as good as you say, I may even like it. Think you can guide these wagons on down there?"

"This ain't the first time I've come down this trail."

"Good. I'm gonna get Nathan, and the two of us'll have a looksee at this place."

Riding through the entrance to Bent's Fort, I could see it was all Dobie had claimed and more. The presence of a war had increased the rapid need for supplies and there were easily four hundred wagons of various shapes and sizes in and around the post. Not to mention elements of Kearney's Army of the West, which, we were told, had arrived only the day before.

"Kind of like a small St. Louis with Indians, ain't it, Finn?"

"Looks to be, brother," I said, taking in the area. "You see anything looks like a billiard hall or something saying such?"

"No. Why?"

I smiled. " 'Cause Dobie says they got a billiard table here, and if they do, there can't be a saloon too far off. I don't know about you, Nathan, but I want to wash the alkali down my throat and see if I've still got the original hide there. Way I figure it, the inside of my throat's got to be either blood-raw or tanned to cure, and right now I don't care which one."

"Know how you feel," Nathan said.

We had walked our mounts all the way to the rear of the fort before spotting it. On the rooftop of the trader's room was the billiard room Tom Dobie had spoken of. I dismounted, handing the reins to Nathan.

"See if you can find some grain for the horses, brother, and check back with me up there," I said, nodding toward the small room on the floor above us.

I had little interest in billiards and made my first request one for something cold. When the man gave me two beers, he started conversing.

"Off the trail, huh?"

"That's a fact," I said, downing half the beer. "I miss my guess, you'll be doing a lot of business before nightfall, friend. There's eight hundred and some thirsty men following the same trail I come in on." I paused, took another sip of my beer. "You get a lot of strangers passing through, I suppose."

"Sure do. Especially since this war flared up. Why?"

"Nothing. Just thought I might see a friend passing through."

"A lot of that going on around here, it seems," the bartender said, looking up from his polished glass.

"Oh? How's that?" All of a sudden I was getting interested in this man's conversation.

"Fella passed through the other day said the same thing."

I froze, felt a cold chill run down my spine as I held the glass motionless before me. "Nervous fella, was he? Kept looking over his shoulder?"

"Yeah," the man said, drawing his answer out. "Could be. I couldn't say for sure, as many as come through here."

When Nathan came in I had already started on the second beer and ordered another for him.

"What's the matter, Finn?" he asked, taking in my face. I never was too good at hiding what I felt when I got mad. "You look like you're ready to fight a grizzly bear."

"Just about, Nathan, just about," I said, not even looking in his direction. "Fact is, I think I found Pa's killer."

"You mean that Garvey character? The one did the backshooting in St. Louis?"

"I think so. Or at least he passed through, according to the barkeep here."

Nathan lowered his voice, glanced cautiously around him before speaking. "You think he knows more about that gold than you give him credit for?"

"It sure looks that way, don't it?" I emptied my glass. "Finish your beer. Dobie and the rest ought to be here any time now, and we're gonna have to find places for 'em to bed down."

The entrance and exit to the billiard room were one and the same, and when we left, the hot afternoon sun nearly blinded me as I walked into its glare. And it almost cost me my life.

"That's him!" I heard a voice shout.

My hand went instinctively to my side, and I was pulling out the Colt as I turned toward the voice, stepping to the side as I did. A shot rang out, and I felt a bullet whisk past me, heard Nathan groan as I brought my gun to bear on Garvey, who was cocking his own weapon a second time. It was a snap-shot I fired, and it caught him just above the belt buckle. He stopped in mid-motion, as if frozen in place, and I fired a quick second shot that hit him in the groin area. Garvey dropped his gun and fell to his side, bent over in pain. As he did,

I brought the Colt to bear on another man only a few feet from Garvey as the stranger began to cock his rifle.

"You can die just as slow as he's doing, sonny!" I yelled as the man paused in hesitation.

"But not as fast as you will if you don't drop that pistol," a voice behind me said as I felt a muzzle of some kind of gun being stuck into my ribs. Nathan was down—of that I was sure—and my own back was to the square. My only chance was to knock the man behind me to his rear and off the rooftop, hoping I could shoot the one to my front before he did the same to me. And for one brief second I found myself wondering if I could do it.

"I don't like Mexican standoffs, mister," Dobie's voice said from the square, loud and clear. "But if that's your game, you're on the wrong end of it."

I glanced over my shoulder, saw the man holding the drop on me looking down into the square as the rifleman before me darted to the side, fleeing. What I saw gave me as much a feeling of relief as it must have fear to the man holding the gun to my back. Tom Dobie sat astride his horse, the ever-present double-barreled shotgun aimed at the gunman next to me. On either side of him were a half-dozen of Doniphan's volunteers, weapons at the ready, led by Doniphan himself.

"I know what you're thinking, son," Dobie said before the man could speak. "You're figuring you could take him and me, or else you think I won't shoot because he's in my line of fire. Well, it don't matter to me, sonny, not one damn bit. All you got to know is that you make one move that don't look right to me and you ain't gonna see today's sunset, much less tomorrow's sunrise. I'm calling the bet, so the next move's yours."

It couldn't have been more than ten seconds between the time Tom Dobie's last words and the time the man dropped the gun from my back, but it seemed an eternity. When I heard the thud of the man's pistol hitting the floor, I took one quick step forward and swung my own Colt in a semicircle, bringing the weapon down on the man's collar. Without a word he fell to the ground, unconscious.

By now the square had filled with curiosity seekers and a number of armed men looking to stop the fracas.

When the group approached Doniphan and his men, it was Tom Dobie who did the talking.

"I saw it all from right here, friend," he said to the leader of the group. "That fella come up behind Callahan after the shootout and was ready to gun him down."

"What about this shootout you're talking about?"

"The son of a bitch threw down on my brother and shot him," I said in a curt voice. "And if that ain't good enough for you, mister, the man killed my Pa back in St. Louis."

"The man's right," Dobie said. "I was there. I seen it."

"We're gonna look into this, Mr. Callahan, or whoever you are, so don't go wandering off. If it checks out, you'll be off the hook, but I wouldn't make a habit of starting trouble like this around here. We don't hold with it."

"I didn't start it, friend," I said in a voice just as hard.

"We'll see about that," the man said before leaving.

Nathan had caught Garvey's slug in the upper left shoulder and rolled off the rooftop onto the ground below when the shooting had started. Luckily, he hadn't been hurt by the fall and the wound was a clean one. We took him to one of the vacant rooms near the trader's rooms, and Lisa brought in her medicine bag and cleaned out his wound.

"You wouldn't really have shot that fella with me standing there like that, would you, Tom?" I asked, watching Lisa.

"Well, now, Finn, that's hard to say." I could tell by the look on his face that I was being set up. "I reckon I probably would have. On the other hand . . . oh, well, it don't matter."

"What do you mean, it don't matter!" I exploded. "I could have got killed if you did that!"

"But you didn't," Dobie said, smiling. "Besides, it's worth seeing the look on your face just knowing you're gonna do some serious thinking on whether I would or wouldn't have. Remember, Finn, I told you I'd get back at you."

"Get back at me?" I didn't understand what he meant.

"Put it this way, hoss," Dobie said as he left the

room. "Maybe next time you'll think twice about throwing someone like Farnsworth at me for hired help."

The next day it was determined that Kearney's Army of the West would stay only so long as it took to resupply at Bent's Fort, then move on to its main objective, the city of Santa Fe.

Nathan took a turn for the worse during the night and Lisa found herself with more than just Ma for a patient, although Ma was more agreeable than Nathan would ever be about it. I had stayed with him as long as I could into the night, then got some shut-eye as Lisa relieved me for a few hours. He had been drifting in and out of consciousness during my stay and I didn't figure he'd come to yet when I returned just before sunrise with some coffee for both Lisa and me. She sat, red-eyed and tired, as I entered the room, but blushing as full as any bride I had ever seen.

"How is he?" I asked, looking down at the sweat-soaked sheets covering my brother.

"Not much better, I'm afraid."

"Are you flushed from exhaustion, or has Nathan been . . . well, you know, kind of—"

"Colorful?" she said, filling in the word I was searching for. "Yes, I think you could say that." She blushed a blood-red again as she said it, but I only smiled.

"You've got to watch out for old Nathan, ma'am," I said, still smiling. "His mind's as hell-bent as the rest of him, and if he gets delirious like this, well, you're liable to hear all sorts of editorializing on the part of his self."

As tired as she was, she managed a smile as she took a sip of coffee. "You two are quite a pair, aren't you?"

"Yes, ma'am, I reckon we are that." I looked down at the passive face of my brother lying there and smiled.

"What's so funny?"

"Oh, I was just thinking. 'Bout Nathan. Hard as he looks and acts, he'll do for you if he takes a liking to you. You can be sure of that, ma'am."

"Lisa. Please, call me Lisa."

"Yes, ma'am." I paused, trying to recall the whole incident, and my grin must have been getting wider.

"Please tell me what's so funny." Her curiosity had

gotten the best of her, like it does most folks when they see mischief about.

"Well, ma'am—uh, Lisa—I do a lot of reading, you see. I reckon reading to me is what drinking or gambling is to some men who take their leisure that way. But I was just thinking of one time way back when. Nathan and me had been out tracking down some hosses that got loose and wound up spending a couple of weeks in the doing of it. Well, Lisa, I'll tell you, I didn't figure to be gone that long, so I left my books and such back at the ranch.

"Anyway, me and Nathan had about out-storied each other, and I happened to mention to him one day how I was about starved for conversation as I was for a good meal. So the whole day we were tracking those horses, why, Nathan kept looking at the horizon. And when we camped for the night, he lit out for that horizon and next thing I know he's bringing in a family in a wagon headed for west Texas."

"Well, that was certainly thoughtful," she said, finishing the last of her coffee. "But I don't understand what's so funny about it."

I smiled. "Lisa, he brought 'em in at gunpoint. Wouldn't let 'em go till they told me everything they knew from three states back."

She put a hand over her mouth, as though to stifle either the beginning of a laugh or a cry. "You're joking," she said. "I mean, he wouldn't—"

"Like I said, ma'am, if he likes you he'll do for you."

I turned to go.

"Finn?"

"Yes, ma'am," I said over my shoulder.

A cautious look came over her face now as she spoke slowly. "What if he *doesn't* like someone?"

"Lisa," I said, telling her the pure and simple truth, "I wouldn't wish that on anyone."

I was loading a pack mule that afternoon when it happened. I had just finished reloading the Conestoga wagon and was trying to figure how best to apportion what seemed to be an enormous amount of supplies on just this one mule. It wasn't that I was tired or sore, like some of the men in the unit. It was just that nothing had

gone right that day since I'd left Nathan and Lisa. Hard
as I tried, I just couldn't concentrate on what needed
doing. And it was mostly the events of the preceding
day that kept me from it.

Somehow, I couldn't shake the feeling that that young
kid—at least that was what I remembered the man with
a rifle as looking like—would try taking another shot at
me. Odds were that if he ran with the likes of Garvey,
he would do just as Garvey would. And I was getting
damn fed up with people taking potshots at me. Hell, it
was enough to make a body believe what that old Mexican had said about death following you around when
you had that gold.

But more than that, I kept mulling over Nathan's
question of the previous day. Did Garvey know more
about the gold than I gave him credit for? If so, then it
seemed logical that he would have a partner somewhere
who would finish the job in case Garvey failed. And that
he did, for Garvey was now dead. But there was something else in the back of my mind, something that kept
tugging at a door that wouldn't open. And it was thinking about that particular subject that sent chills down my
spine.

And that's when it happened.

"You shouldn't have done that to me, bud," a voice
from the side said. I turned to see the man who had held
the gun to my back the day before, the one I had sliced
along the side of the head when Dobie had the drop on
him. I noticed then that he was of medium build and
shorter than me, but his muscles were powerful in the
compact body. Several scars on the naked upper half of
his body were witness to the fact that the man was no
newcomer to fighting. I also noticed that he had no
weapon; but then, he probably didn't need one.

Or maybe it was because of the two walking toward
me from the other side, for they were armed. One carried a Colt Paterson, the other some sort of dueling
pistol. Both had them drawn and pointed right toward
my midsection.

"I never did take kindly to anyone sticking a gun in
my back," I said, realizing at once that the only weapon
I had on me was the bowie knife, for I had removed the
Colt in order to load the supplies. And an empty water

gourd. Most people don't think of much more than guns and knives when you mention weapons to them, but you'd be surprised what kind of weapons there are around you that you don't even know about. "You know, friend, you keep making small mistakes and sooner or later they all add up to one big mistake," I said, trying to sound casual as I slowly refilled the gourd with water. And I'll tell you, friend, that can be mighty hard when you get scared.

What must have been two of their henchmen suddenly appeared from the side alley of the trader's room. Both were big and ugly and had the kind of sneer on their faces that said they were spoiling for a fight. Somehow they didn't surprise me as much as the emergence from the trader's room itself of the young man who had been with Garvey the day before. He leaned his rifle against the wall, next to the door, then slowly walked toward me as the others did the same. Now, it didn't take much to see that I was going to wind up looking like some piece of butchered meat if I didn't get out of there right quick, and I never did take a liking to busted ribs and such. On the other hand, if these fellas had a hand in the shooting of my brother, well, they could have a piece of me if they liked. But I was going to make sure that by the time they were through I had me a piece of them, too.

"Boys, you just stepped in it," I said, giving a quick glance to the ground at the feet of the two with their guns drawn. There was cow pie and horse apples all over the place, and I was hoping to get their attention. I did. When they looked down, I tossed the water in the eyes of the one with the Colt, then swung the gourd down on his partner's single-shot pistol, setting it off. That pistol going off like that should have let a whole bunch of people know what was going on, but I didn't have time to wait. The edge of the gourd caught the wet one on his nose and I whacked him alongside the head with it a second time, breaking it. Like I said, you can use just about anything for a weapon, and poking that fella's partner in the eye sort of took the tough out of him. He let out a scream like I'd never heard before and I knew I'd gotten some more attention.

I was about to face one of the ugly ones from the alley

then when I felt a series of hard, fast blows to my side that nearly made me sick. Spinning around, I saw the sawed-off ruffian just before he threw a left and a right into my side again. I thought I felt something crack, but before I could recover, I found myself flying backwards from the force of two more punches. And the next thing I knew, I was flat on my back, each of the ugly ones sitting on an arm as the muscular little fighter landed on my chest and looked down at me with a sneer.

"Tough nut, are ye, lad?" he said with a jeer. "We'll see about that." Then he lifted his fist, but the blow never came, for a huge red blur filled the background behind him.

"Betcher ass, Charlie," I heard Doniphan say loudly as one of his ham-sized hands grasped the ruffian around the neck and physically lifted him off of me. The body went sailing through the air, and I heard a dull thud next to where the Conestoga was.

As quickly as he had surprised the first man, one of his enormously oversized feet shot out, and one of the plug-uglies did a somersault, freeing my right arm. By God, this fellow Doniphan was worse to be around when he got mad than Nathan! I spit in the third man's face and swung as hard as I could, hitting him alongside the ear. His eyes turned to a glaze as he slowly fell forward and I rolled to my side, then got on my feet.

Doniphan had his hand around the muscular little ruffian's neck, bashing his head into the side of my wagon, and for some reason I found myself wondering if he wouldn't damage the wagon doing it. It was then the two would-be gunmen rushed us from the rear. I turned in time enough to catch one by the shoulder. I spun him around and hit him twice in the face, sending him reeling. It was the third blow, a roundhouse punch to the jaw, that knocked him out. Throwing that last one hurt me as much as it did him, for I could feel it all the way down to my rib cage.

The second man had gotten past me, and I could only hope that Doniphan could handle him himself. But what I heard and saw left no doubt in my mind that this gigantic Missourian would never have any trouble taking care of himself. The whole sight seemed comedic more than anything else. Apparently, the man had hit Doniphan a blow to the back, expecting him to sink to the ground. Instead, the big man turned toward his rear, and I swear I could see the fire in that orange-colored hair standing on end!

"Goddamnit, that hurt!" was all he said as he grabbed his attacker by the shirtfront in one hand, held him at arm's-length and in two blows broke the man's jaw and nose. When he let loose the shirtfront, the body dropped to the ground, as lifeless as the first man he had taken up with. Doniphan only frowned and shook his head as he watched the man fall. "Sorry bastards," he said to no one in particular. "Never make it in the First Missouri."

The shot had drawn a crowd, but only a few had come from the trader's room, and when I glanced in that direction, the young rifleman was still standing there, an observer of the free-for-all. He stopped enjoying it when our eyes met. He had that same look of fear as I'd seen in him the day before, and just like the day before, he turned to run. But when he did, it was toward his rifle, stacked next to the door of the trader's room.

"Don't do it!" I yelled, drawing my bowie knife as I said it. I didn't throw it until I saw the young man reach for his rifle. A quick glance was all he gave me, but I could see in his eyes that he wanted out of the situation and was willing to kill to get away. The knife landed hilt-deep in his side, and he slumped to the floor of the boardwalk, his grip on the rifle slackening.

There was a pool of blood forming under him as I yanked my knife from his body, watched him grimace as I did so, knowing he was dying. I wiped the blood off on his pants leg and stuck the blade back in its sheath.

"You're crazy!" the lad said with conviction. "Garvey was right! You're crazy!" There was a wildness in his eyes now, and he knew he was dying. Slowly shaking his head, he stared at me, frowning. "He never even . . . he said he never did—" Then his head slumped to his side.

Doniphan grabbed me by the arm, yanking me away as though I were cemented to the spot where I stood.

"Let's get out of here, Callahan," he said. "Looks to me like you're losing your popularity around here faster than most."

He wasn't far from wrong either, for there were some angry-looking men converging on the sight of all this bloodshed, and they didn't look like they were wanting any explanations. It was then I recalled Shakespeare's saying about discretion being the better part of valor. So, without appearing to look like we were trying to get the hell out of there, I tied the pack mule to the wagon while Doniphan and a couple of his boys tossed the half-dozen boxes of supplies into the Conestoga. From the looks on the faces of some of those men, I'd say it was a miracle we got the wagon and us out the gates and to our camp.

"Callahan, do you always make a habit of getting in this much trouble?" Doniphan asked when we pulled into camp.

"Not if I can help it," I said, wincing as I got down from the wagon, suddenly remembering the bones I thought I had heard crack. "But I wouldn't talk if I was you, hoss. From what I seen you do back there, I've got a feeling you'd have started the ball if those hardcases didn't. Seems to me you were having a right good time of it," I said, half smiling.

"Just having some fun, Callahan," he said, returning my smile while he rubbed a hand on his own backside. "Just having some fun."

According to the doctor, my ribs were in worse shape than I thought. "Son, you've got some bad bruises that are gonna turn into fractures if you don't take it easy for a bit," the leathery-faced old man said. He was wrapping my lower chest as tight as he could when a rider came galloping into camp from the direction of the fort. And he surely was in a hurry, the way he left that horse at a run, pulling up in front of Doniphan like that.

"We got trouble, boss," the young rider said, all excited.

"Whoa, Jim," Doniphan said, holding a cautious hand up. "Settle down, son, and catch your breath." One of the strange quirks this fiery red-haired man had was calling his men either Jim or Charlie, regardless of whether he knew their names or not. I'd not seen it before in a man but wouldn't argue the point. "Now, what's this about trouble?"

The rider threw an angry glance in my direction.

"It's him," he said, his eyes now glaring with hatred. "I don't know what he done, but there's a handful of men in there," he said, yanking a thumb over his shoulder at the post, "that are saying he killed a man in cold blood. If he's the one that's got a stove-up brother, then they got him and the rest of his family under guard in one of them rooms. Ain't letting 'em go till he turns hisself in, they're saying."

I got up and walked over to Doniphan and his messenger. The thought of having my family held captive wasn't a pleasant one, and I found myself forgetting the pain in my side.

"But that ain't the worst, Colonel," the young man continued as I approached.

"Oh?" Doniphan cocked an eye toward the speaker, and I knew he had taken more than a casual interest in the lad's story.

"No, sir. Them fellas are claiming the First Missouri ain't gonna get it's supplies less'n we turn Callahan in."

"Wait a minute, son," Doniphan said, a slow frown now forming on his face. "Does Charlie Bent know about this?"

"No, sir. It's just this bunch of men."

"Well, I'll tell you what, son. If Charlie Bent is anything like I've been hearing, he's gonna use these pilgrims for cannon fodder when he gets his hands on 'em. Half-dozen or so, you say?"

"Yes, sir."

"Two of 'em look like they been walked on by Sarah's mule?"

For the first time, the young rider smiled. "Yes, sir."

"That's our boys," I said and Doniphan nodded.

"Don't you worry about our supplies, son," the big man said. "We'll have 'em."

"But what about him, sir?" The rider nodded toward me.

Doniphan was silent a moment, then the frown turned to a grin as he glanced at me as though reading my thoughts.

"Well, son, I reckon if it's Callahan they want, then we ought to give him to 'em."

* * *

There wasn't a full moon that night, and it was just as well, for it enabled us to pass through the main gate without any trouble after dark. It was just me, Doniphan and a handful of his men who went in. Most of the activity for the night had moved from the large square to indoor adobe rooms where relaxation took precedence over the more serious events of the day, and for that I was thankful.

Doniphan had the young courier along to point out the men in the group he'd said would be holding my family. But we wouldn't have needed him, for it was hard to miss where they were keeping the hostages. There were four men outside the room, two on each side of the door, one each at the sides of the building. The two guards at the front door came to a quick port arms when they saw me, my hands behind my back, flanked by Doniphan and the young rider, who had his pistol drawn, covering me.

"You can put them away, boys," Doniphan said as they neared. "I got him bound up good enough." When the guards frowned at one another, he added, "Well, you said you wanted Callahan, right? You did tell Jim here that's what you wanted, didn't you?"

The heavier of the two shrugged. "I reckon."

"Well, I always deliver, boys," Doniphan said, smiling. "Always."

Before the guards could figure out what it was the gigantic Missourian was smiling at, they were staring into two pistol barrels, the one held by "Jim" and my own.

"They ain't gonna do you no good, friend," I said as one of the men gave a quick glance at the guards in the alley beside the guest room. And when he did, he saw I was right, for each of them was standing stock-still. They moved only when Doniphan waved his arm. Then the guards marched forward, each with one of Doniphan's men behind him.

"Now, don't be bashful, boys," I said. "I want to know who else is in there besides my family."

The heavyset guard may have been the stronger of the two, but I could see he was the most scared, too, when a cold sweat broke out on his forehead. "Just Ferrel and Monk," he volunteered.

"Ferrel and Monk?" I surveyed the faces of the four men, then turned to Doniphan. "That'd be Ugly and the sawed-off runt that thinks he's a descendant of Napoleon."

Doniphan grabbed the rifles from both guards, handing them to the rider. "Here, Jim, you take these and let me have that Colt of yours." He had that little bit of craziness in him now, and I knew that, like it or not, Doniphan was going into that room with me.

"I'm gonna take whoever's on the right," I said. "You cover the left."

"Sure thing, Callahan."

When he kicked the door in, one of the hinges snapped and it flew off at an angle. I rushed in quickly, moving off to the right and bringing my Walker Paterson to bear on Monk, the short, muscular man I had confronted earlier.

"Do it and you're dead, mister" was all I said as the man was about to bring his rifle to his shoulder. When he saw I would kill him without a second thought, he set the rifle down, leaning it against the wall.

I was suddenly made aware of Doniphan's entrance as I heard a commotion behind me. In a quick glance I saw Doniphan bring down a hamlike fist on the ugly one's face, heard him crash to the floor.

"Improved his looks already," Doniphan said.

"You all right, Ma?" She had taken Nathan's place in the lone bed in the room, but aside from being scared some she looked none the worse for wear. Nathan sat on a stool next to the bed, half-conscious and leaning on the headboard for support.

"The women are fine, Finn," Tom Dobie said, walking from the corner of the room and picking up Monk's rifle. "But they wouldn't have been if you hadn't showed up."

"How's that?"

"Seems these two figured to have some fun with Lisa, Ellie and your Ma," Dobie said, his voice hard through gritted teeth.

"Please, Finn," Ma said when she saw my face get as hard as Dobie's. "No more bloodshed. You know how I despise it."

"Sure, Ma," I said slowly, never taking my eyes from Monk. "You know I wouldn't do anything to upset you." I felt the grip on the Colt tighten as a sudden urge to shoot Monk came over me. But Dobie soon covered him with his shotgun and I lowered the Colt. It was then I saw a faint glimpse of a grin come to Monk's face and, hoss, that tore it! "Like hell!" I said and brought the Colt up alongside the man's head, drawing blood from his ear. When he fell, I tossed the pistol to my left hand, kneeled down beside the man and drew the bowie knife from its sheath. I put the razor edge of the knife at the corner of the man's mouth as a look of fear came to Monk's face.

"You wipe that smile from your face, you worthless vermin, or I'll cut it off!" The fear on his face was now complete as his complexion turned a sheet-white. "Told you, sonny, you keep making those small mistakes and they wind up being one big mistake. And you just made your last one," I said, applying a slight pressure to the corner of his mouth.

"No! Please!"

"Hold on, Callahan," Doniphan said, placing a firm hand on my shoulder. His grip loosened when I gave him a hard look. "Let it be, Finn. You got your piece of him." Then he looked past me at the young ruffian on the floor. "Charlie, I'd get the hell outta this profession, was I you. The way you go about it, it ain't gonna get you nothing but dead before you're old enough to brag about it."

"He's right, Finn," Dobie said.

"Look, Finn," Doniphan said, "seems to me it's you and your brother have got more to lose than these scum. Besides, you ain't just too awful popular around here right now. Ask me, I'd say you best skedaddle for a bit until things cool down."

"What about Ma?" Nathan asked, speaking for the first time since the incident occurred. He appeared to be only half-conscious, but even then he was still looking out for Ma and Ellie.

"Don't you worry none about your Mama," Doniphan said. "I figure that between Dobie here and my volunteers, well, they ain't none of these scalawags gonna do any harm to us." Then he turned to me. "You just take off for the hills or horizon, whichever is closest, and do some outriding for a while, and one of us will let you know when it's safe to return to camp."

"How about it, Nathan?" I asked. "You up to riding?"

I wasn't about to admit that my own side wasn't feeling all that good, so when Nathan nodded assent, I tried to be as encouraging as possible. "Good. Can you be ready to ride in half an hour?"

"Right, Finn," he said and in his own clumsy way began gathering what he thought he'd need.

"Ma, I'll be back as soon as I can," I said, bending down to kiss her. "Lisa, you take care of her."

Lisa smiled. "You bet, Finn."

"Same with you," I said, giving Ellie a quick kiss. "Take care of yourself." She smiled briefly, and for a moment I thought she was going to cry.

Tom Dobie followed me outside, but I made sure we were away from the others before I spoke to him.

"You know it ain't just the women I want you looking after, don't you?"

"I figured you'd get around to that before you left. Yeah, I remember what you've got on your mind, Callahan."

"By the way, where was Farnsworth when all this was happening?"

"Search me. He probably found a hole to crawl into when he got news of the fighting."

Lisa was standing in the doorway, giving Nathan instructions along with a bottle of something.

"Take this at least once a day, and it'll keep the fever down and infection out of the wound," she said in an authoritative voice.

"The original snake oil," Nathan said, taking the bottle from her with a forced smile. "Guaranteed to kill you or cure you."

We were just outside the gate when a dark figure stepped from the shadows. I never did get used to surprises, so it wasn't long before I had a Colt in my hand again.

"No! Don't shoot! It's me," Farnsworth said.

"Now, what the hell are you doing out here?" I asked.

"Well, sir, Mr. Dobie said you had to leave, and I thought you might be able to use this," he said, producing a bottle of some sort of whiskey. "I understand the nights get very cold."

I took the bottle, held the liquid up to the dim evening light. It was likely Taos Lightning or some kind of concoction that was just as effective as the snake oil Nathan had.

"Well, now, Farnsworth, I reckon you might get the hang of this country yet." I holstered the pistol and offered him my hand. "Much obliged, hoss."

"Luck to you, sir."

"Farnsworth, I don't believe in luck. People make their own."

"Yes, sir."

"But thanks anyway."

We mounted our horses and took off for the mountains then, a pack mule trailing behind us.

It was close to a month before Nathan or I saw our family again.

Chapter 17

It was mid-December by the time all of the elements of Doniphan's command came together once more. By then Nathan and I were back with Ma and the others, the authorities at Bent's Fort far behind us now.

We were near Valverde now, the most southerly settlement in the territory, and in a way I was glad, for it was here that we met up with some three hundred traders with wagonloads of supplies. They cared little about the war and, they claimed, were headed for Chihuahua with goods originally purchased in St. Louis. With that in mind, I pulled up behind the Conestoga carrying Ma. She might be as strong as she was always putting on to be, but the fact of the matter was that no matter how tough a woman you were, giving birth to a child in the wilderness could take a toll on a woman. It had been that way when Ellie had James, and by my recollections, Ma wasn't far off from having her time.

"Lisa," I said, pulling back the flap on the wagon.

"Yes." She looked up from Ma's side, and for a moment I had the notion she might have been crying.

"Get James's horse and come with me. I found us one of these wagons that have medicines and such. And you know more about 'em than I do."

I don't know if saying that gave her a new sense of usefulness or what, but she looked a whole sight happier when she got on that horse. When we got there, the wagon master began showing her the various types of medication he had and she began to pick and choose them sparingly. By the time she was through, Nathan had ridden up, and I handed him a box to put the bottles in.

"More snake oil?"

"If it is, it had better be triple-X for what I'm paying," I said, which made Nathan smile. He had mostly recovered from his wound and was a part of the adventure again, throwing in his two cents' worth on how everything should be run. That also meant he could be a pain in the neck located about three feet lower at times, but with Nathan I wouldn't have it any other way. What the hell—he was my brother.

But that didn't do much for another problem I had on my mind, and that was Lisa Harris and the naive way she had of looking at things out here. She seemed to know everything about medicine and nothing about frontier life, and I figured it was time she knew.

"You love Tom Dobie, don't you?" I asked as we slowly walked our mounts back to Ma's wagon.

It was a question she didn't expect, and she nearly dropped a bottle before she recovered. Then a slow, shy smile came to her face.

"Yes. Very much. Why do you ask?"

I shrugged, searching for the right words so I could get my point across without hurting her. "Curiosity, I reckon." I noticed that Nathan was having no part in this conversation, acting as though he were minding his own business. "It'd be rough if you stayed. This land is hell on women. Don't offer much in the way of a future."

She toyed with the bottle for a bit before turning to me. "Are you sure, Finn? Are you really sure? Who's to say just who does and doesn't survive out here, anyway? Look at Farnsworth," she said. "He's turning into a pretty useful person. So who's to say?" When she stopped abruptly, I could tell by the look on her face that she was mulling over whether or not to say what was on her mind, and when she spoke next it was with a faltering hint of bravery. "It seems to me that you men have it a lot easier than the women out here."

"Oh?" Nathan said, taking a new interest in our talk.

"Well, sure. You two and Tom and the rest of these yahoos go around acting tough and talk about fighting these Mexicans like you're having some kind of fun. Then when you find a woman, you expect her to show you all sorts of tenderness and love, but—" She broke off in what sounded like pure frustration.

"But what?" I asked.

"But you never even think about what else she goes through for you," she said in what almost sounded like a pleading tone. "Do you ever think of how tough she has to be when she's patching you up and you're that close to dying? Or . . ." She paused again, not looking away but staring right past me to Nathan, a tear rolling down her cheek. "Or waiting for you when you go off to fight those silly damn wars you fun about, not knowing if you'll ever come back? No, I doubt that there's much of a future out here for me," she said, wiping her nose with a sleeve and turning back to me, "but I'll stay, Finn. Maybe loving him is a crazy reason to, but it's the only one I've got."

"That's mighty bold talk for a woman ain't been out here that long," Nathan said, irritation in his voice. "Where'd you hear talk like that?"

"From Ellie." Right about then, I don't believe I've ever seen two more confused people in my life. Nathan couldn't believe what he was hearing, and Lisa couldn't believe he didn't know. "I thought you knew," she said in a slow, apologetic manner.

"No," Nathan said just as slowly. "I didn't."

I was hard put to find words for the occasion, so I spent the rest of the ride in silence, as did Nathan and Lisa. I didn't know much about Tom Dobie, but as long as Nathan and I had been on the frontier, it seemed to be one long fight after another to keep our affairs in order. If it wasn't Comanches, it was Mother Nature and Father Time, always something. About that Lisa was right, for my brother and I had been in more than one fight where one or the other of us had gotten shot up some. And Ellie had sure done enough patching up to be a nurse and doctor her own self, but she never did speak much of those times. She was dependable and never asked much. I'll say that for her. The more I thought of it, the more I got to wondering if what Lisa had said didn't have some truth to it after all.

Lisa tied her mount to the back of the wagon, and I handed her a box of medicinals.

"You'll do Tom good," I said. "And what you said back there, well, you might just have something."

Nathan handed her a second, smaller box and reined his horse toward the front of the wagon. I wasn't far behind him and saw him reach up and grab Ellie by the arm, pulling her down to him and kissing her long and hard.

I don't know if it was the shock of being kissed out in the open like that or seeing me sitting astride my horse and smiling at them that made Ellie blush, but she did.

"Good Lord, Nathan," she said in a state of shock after he released her, "what was that about?"

Nathan had that same look about him that I'd seen ten years earlier when he and Ellie first met—that same cockeyed look in his eyes that said he'd found someone he liked an awful lot.

"I never could win an argument with a woman," he said with a smile and wheeled his horse to the side, gone in an instant. Ellie now had a perplexed but somewhat happy look on her face. It was the kind that said she wanted to know more, and it was me she glanced at next.

"Beats the hell outta me," I said and put the heels to my horse before I got in any more trouble.

The traders decided to join us, figuring they had the same goal in mind as we did, just for a different purpose. And most of us knew what that was. The goods they'd bought in St. Louis could be sold for as much as ten times their original price, but under the circumstances the Mexican government would be charging $360 a ton for a duties tax on their freight. So with Doniphan and his men charged with the taking of Chihuahua, most of those traders figured they only stood to gain by having an armed force accompany them.

A head count of the First Missouri still showed some eight hundred men. And the addition of the freighters, teamsters and others in camp just added that much more confidence to the men, one of them making the statement that this lash-up could "whip anything this side of Chihuahua." In fact, it gave them so much confidence that they were soon calling themselves "Doniphan's Thousand."

But those lads had every bit of their confidence put to the test when we set out on what one Spanish-speaking fella I'd met called the *Jornada del Muerte*, the "Journey of Death." It took us three days to cross the ninety miles of desert that contained only one small water hole. But lack of water was only one of our hardships. It was mid-December, and the water, when we found it, was more often than not frozen. The summer heat had quickly disappeared, replaced by the freezing winter weather and fierce, heavy winds that accompanied it. To build a fire was near impossible, for this portion of the desert was barren of wood of any type.

Game was as scarce as the wood needed to cook it properly, but I produced what you might call a veritable feast one afternoon when I did find some. That jackrabbit was tough and stringy, but you can bet Nathan, I and the rest thought a good deal of it while we chewed away. We had fixed the women's supper first, and it was one they thought right tasty, too. We never did tell them that what they were eating was fried rattlesnake. All Nathan and I were concerned about then was that Ma keep up her strength, and I remember times we brought game in that was so small a portion we passed it up just to make sure she had her share.

Dona Ana was the small Mexican town we came upon at the end of that three-day trek, and you couldn't have found another group of men so relieved to see it as Doniphan's. There was forage for the horses and corn meal and dried fruit for the men as they rested. It was also during that rest that we came on word that there were enemy troops nearing our area.

I never was sure just where the information came from, but it seemed there were some two thousand dragoons to the south of us at a place called El Paso del Norte. It was also said they were looking for "*norte-americanos*." If the information was correct, they also had four cannons with them. That meant that Doniphan and his men were outnumbered at just better than two to one, but it sure didn't seem to bother those boys. Fact is, they were getting real uppity and acting like they were just spoiling for a fight, no matter what the odds. And you couldn't blame them in a way. Hell, who'd want to go through the journey we'd just been through to be told that the war was over? But Farnsworth was still an easterner in his thinking and couldn't understand it one lick.

"I can't figure it out," he said when I mentioned the enthusiasm of the men. "There are two thousand well-armed enemy troops in the area and these men are anxious to engage them? Why, they must be daft!"

"Can't say as I blame 'em," Tom Dobie said, hitching up a team of oxen.

"Then you're as daft as they are!" the drummer said.

Dobie stopped what he was doing, put his hands on his hips and looked down at the smaller man.

"Farnsworth, let me tell you something. These men signed up for one year of volunteering to fight a war. They've had no pay, no supplies and damn little direction. This is gonna be their first run-in with the Mexicans, so I can understand how they feel. So far all they've done is march a thousand miles and complain. You've got to realize one thing."

"What's that?"

"Where most of them come from, proving yourself in a good fight makes all the complaining worth it. Now, let's get these teams hitched. We've got to git these wagons rolling."

It was the third day after we left Dona Ana that Ma went into labor. Lisa and Ellie stayed with her while James drove the wagon.

"She says she'll have it by sunset," Lisa said when I asked how Ma was doing. "She sounds pretty definite about it, almost as if she can tell."

"That's your department more than mine," I said.

Nathan, I and some of the others scouted forward during the day, searching out wood and good grass for the animals once Doniphan decided to call a halt for the night. It was midafternoon when we came upon a clearing alongside a little island of the Rio Grande. It would have been perfect for a camping area but for one thing— the enemy soldiers on the other side.

"Looks like we're all gonna have a rough day," Nathan said.

"Well, folks," one of Doniphan's men said, "it ain't

rumor no more. Looks to be a good two thousand of 'em.''

Nathan was checking his loads, but I already knew what he had in mind.

"Hoss," I said to one of the men who had been a frequent rider with us, "you get that wagon of ours up to that clearing someplace by the remuda and some of those supply wagons. It'll be close to the shooting, but at least we'll have cover from two sides, and that's better than nothing." Then to another I said, "You find me that sawbones that calls himself a doctor and get him to the wagon right quick-like. I got a feeling Ma's gonna need him more than Doniphan and his men."

Dobie and Farnsworth soon arrived, and we filled them in on the situation and left the others, heading for our wagon. Nathan was rubbing his arm when he dismounted, but I could tell it wasn't the arm that was bothering. A frown came to his face as James got down from the wagon, walked to the rear and began untying the reins of his horse.

"And where do you think you're going?" Nathan asked.

"With you," the boy said simply, as if it was the natural thing to do.

"Not hardly," his father said in a sterner tone this time.

"But Pa," the boy pleaded.

"Look, son, your mother and Lisa are gonna be too busy tending to your grandmother to keep an eye out for their own selves, and I need someone to do it and you're it." Then a hint of mischief crossed his face as he looked back and forth at Dobie and me. "Besides, if I leave Finn back here, he's likely to get out one of those books of his and forget all about watching the women. And God only knows what'll happen if I leave Dobie and Lisa in the same area for more'n five minutes."

I smiled at Nathan's sense of humor, but Tom Dobie was slowly turning a crimson red from the neck up, his grip on the shotgun visibly tightening. "One of these days, Callahan. One of these days."

When we left, we agreed that Dobie and Farnsworth should keep an eye on the remuda as well as the wagon in case something did happen and James found himself in more hot water than he could handle.

When we got to the front, the Mexican army wasn't half a mile away, forming a line of battle. Watching them, I had the same feeling I had had down at Palo Alto when the Mexican army had prepared to meet Taylor's men.

Shortly, a messenger from the enemy force rode forward, carrying the black flag with the motto *Libertad o Muerte*, "Liberty or Death." He stopped midway in the field, and we watched as Doniphan himself rode out to meet the man. The exchange was a brief one as both men headed back to their own forces. When he rode up, Doniphan was besieged by anxious men wanting to know what had taken place. He had that arrogant look about him that he handled so well when he was mad, so I wasn't sure if the news was good or bad.

"Son of a bitch said if we didn't surrender, he was gonna take us and give no quarter."

"What did you tell him, Colonel?"

Doniphan cocked an eye toward the man who had spoken, and a sneer came to his face. "Told the bastards to charge and be damned!"

A chorus of cheers went up as the men realized that they were finally going to be in their long-awaited fight. But the only thing crossing my mind as I watched them was the fate of that young Ranger at Palo Alto who had wanted to fight so badly and who had died so quickly on the battlefield. It made me wonder how many of these boys would never see the end of the day.

When the cheering died down, Doniphan instructed his men.

"Line up enough so's we got 'em covered and give 'em a good hundred-and-fifty-yards lead. Then show 'em why we always got meat on the table back in Missouri."

The big man likely wasn't aware of it, and I've a notion that if he was he wouldn't have cared, but the truth was that we only had around five hundred of his men on hand to do the fighting then. Throughout the whole journey, the various companies of Doniphan's Thousand had been spread out over a distance of march that often covered several miles. That pushed the odds up to four-to-one, but it didn't seem to bother these men at all as they dismounted and prepared for battle. Our horses were led out of rifle range when the Mexicans began to charge.

The enemy infantry was only a quarter-mile away when they first fired on the Missourians, but those rounds fell far short of their objective. I'll say this much. Those backwoods boys may not have been soldiers, but they sure knew how to follow orders, for they waited until the Mexicans were 150 yards away before they started shooting. And lordy, did they open the ball! Those riflemen let out a withering fire that totally shocked the Mexican forces. For fifteen minutes we held those infantrymen in check with our fire, and you can believe that the way they were getting killed off, well, hoss, they were having serious second thoughts about advancing any closer to our lines!

Nathan was using that Hawken of his, while I had a Colt revolving rifle I had dug out of the wagon. Both were effective long guns, but with all that gunsmoke in the air, it sure did get hard to find a target sometimes. Nathan never was much for having patience and fired up his powder and ball as fast as he could. Me, I taken my time and made them count, and most of them did. But it was Nathan who pulled out his Walker Paterson and went to firing hell-for-leather even when the Mexicans were out of range. The man was purely frustrated. That I could see.

"What's the matter, Nathan?" I asked, reloading the Colt rifle. "Losing your touch?"

"Hell, no!" He shook his head in disgust, looked down at his pistol. "I tell you, Finn, I got to get a bigger gun. Can't hit nothing with this forty-one no more."

I smiled, knowing full well Nathan was a perfectionist about his marksmanship. But the smile faded as quickly as it had appeared as I looked past Nathan.

The Mexican dragoons had broken from the right flank and were heading for the parked wagon trains. And the wagons they were heading for were ours!

Nathan was cussing a blue streak as he reloaded his pistol. I said, "Here!" and tossed the Colt revolving rifle to him and quick-like reached for the extra Colt in my *mochila*, long since emptied of its gold.

"What the—"

"The wagons!" I yelled and dug my heels into my mount, totally forgetting the enemy soldiers to our front. Right now I was concerned with the ones who were threatening my family.

The wagons were close to a hundred yards away, out of pistol range, especially for a man a-horse, so I saved my six shots for targets I knew I could hit. With all the shooting going on, the only shots I was listening for were the ones from our wagon. The first one came as one of three Mexicans approached the wagon from the rear, one of them pulling back the flap and taking a step in. A shot rang out, and I was hoping it was the old Paterson Nathan had left behind for James. My hopes were confirmed only an instant following the shot as the Mexican soldier flew backwards and out of the wagon, dead. I remember thinking for a split second that this James was going to be another by God Callahan, for he had as many surprises in him as his grandfather had had! But this was no time for patting anyone on the back, not yet. James was sticking his head out the back of the wagon, and there were still the dead Mex's two companions to take care of, not to mention what looked like a bunch more off to the side that wanted a piece of this fandango.

Then a whole bunch of things sort of happened at once, like they always do. Thinking back, you can never be sure which one happened first, but then, it usually doesn't matter. A handful of teamsters and traders took to cutting those advancing enemy soldiers to pieces like they were so many ribbons and it was decoration day and they were in need. But three more in the lead had gotten past them and were heading for those two by the wagons.

That was when Dobie and Farnsworth materialized. They seemed to come out of nowhere. Dobie looked right at home, leveling his scattergun at two of the advancers and doing them in right on the spot. But Farnsworth was looking anything but heroic now, simply standing there near the edge of our wagon, limply holding a musket in his hands.

"Goddamnit, Farnsworth, use it!" I heard Dobie yell as one of the soldiers took a slice at James's arm with a knife as the boy looked on, almost as helpless now as the drummer. Maybe it was seeing that happen to James that did it—I never will know for sure—but it was then that Farnsworth stepped forward and stuck the musket in the man's side and pulled the trigger, sending the body to the ground.

That was also the same time that Nathan and I got within range. I slid off that horse at a run and fired at and hit the third enemy soldier who had gotten past Dobie. I taken him out just as he was about to do in Farnsworth, but the drummer never even noticed the body fall. He was too horrified at the sight of the man he had just killed. I heard another rifle crack and saw Nathan shoot one of the others trying to get near the camp. Then the shooting stopped, at least in our area, and the enemy seemed to fade from sight.

"Mr. Farnsworth!" James said in surprise, oblivious to the blood on his arm. "You shot him!"

"Yes," the drummer said, looking down at the body. "I killed a man." Then his face turned as white as a sheet as he dropped the blood-stained rifle and brought a hand to his mouth, running toward the far side of the wagon as he did.

"What the hell's the matter with him?" Dobie asked as he finished reloading his shotgun.

"He just saved my life," James said in awe. "He killed a man to save my life." Seeing the little drummer gun down a man wasn't anything he or any of the rest of us ever expected to see.

"Don't look like you did too bad yourself," I said, looking down at the pool of blood surrounding the dead Mexican. "Come on, let's get that arm of yours taken care of before you bleed to death."

"Finn," I heard him say, looking at all of the carnage in the area.

"What?"

"How come it don't feel right? All this?"

I remembered my own feelings about killing my first man back at San Jacinto. Oh, I had taken one out of the saddle earlier when Cooper Hansen and me had caught up with Nathan, but it was seeing all that blood all over the place and knowing that one of those bodies lying there might be the one you had killed, it was seeing that that made me ask myself the same thing James was now.

"It never does, James. It never does." I looked into the scared blue eyes of the shaken boy. "And if you're lucky, it never will."

It was then we heard the cry come from inside the wagon. It was the cry of a newborn baby, and by God, he sure did sound healthy!

Compared to some battles, this one was more like a skirmish, but then, it gets kind of hard to convince a man that he ain't fighting a battle when his life is on the line and he just might lose it. And any one of those Missouri boys would tell you it was a battle, even if it did only last a half an hour. Someone called it the Battle of El Brazito, something to do with the place we were at, but that didn't matter much to us right then. You see, Doniphan and Nathan and I and the rest of those boys, well, we never give a hoot one way or another what you call a fight or how long it is by your timekeeper. No matter how many fights or skirmishes or battles or whatever you want to call them a man gets into, well, there is only one thing a body is sure of then, and that is that when he's out there doing battle . . . well, damn, but if it don't seem like the longest time of his life.

According to Doniphan, we had killed at least forty-three of the enemy and wounded "one hell of a lot more." Our own casualties were seven wounded, none of them fatally. The important thing was that the Mexicans were in full retreat and we were no longer in danger.

It was after he had taken his body count that Doniphan rode with us to the wagon. Nearly everyone was inside looking after Ma for one silly reason or another, knowing full well they were looking for an excuse to see the newborn child.

"I understand there was quite a bit going on back here, too, this afternoon," Doniphan said with a smile.

"Oh, yes, Mr. Doniphan," Ma said. Then, glancing at James, she added, "It seems my grandson has taken up saving ladies for a trade." Then, taking James's hand in her own, she squeezed it. "I'm most proud of him."

"Don't blame you. But who's the new recruit?" the

big man asked, motioning toward the sleeping bundle in her arms. "Just so's I can add him to my list of volunteers, you know."

"Yeah, Meg," Lisa said excitedly. "I forgot all about that. You've got three boys now. What are you gonna name this one?"

"Well, I don't know," she said, and I could see her drift back into the past for a moment before speaking. "As I recall, when my first son was born, I wanted to name him John, but Liam thought so highly of Nathan Hale that he named him that instead. And when my second son was born . . . well, Finnian seemed so appropriate."

"And Irish," Doniphan added.

"Yes," Ma said with a smile. "And I suppose I've still got a bit of the old Irish in me. You know, Mr. Doniphan, my husband put a value on the men he thought great. If he hadn't, Nathan wouldn't have his name. And had he lived long enough to meet you, I'm sure he would have liked you, for you're the same individualist he was. Would you do me an honor, Mr. Doniphan?"

"Ma'am?" The big Missourian was caught off guard.

"It occurs to me, Mr. Doniphan, that I might just be able to have everything I want in this son. I still like the name John, but I like the Irish version, Sean, even better, so that will be his name. And Donovan. Sean Donovan Callahan will be his full name. And each time I see him, I'll remember not only Liam and the greatness he saw in men, but that oversized, oafishly dressed Missourian who somehow got us as far as he did before I had my son."

Doniphan's complexion quickly turned a bright shade of orange that nearly matched his hair, and for a moment I thought the man was about to lose his nerve.

"Well, uh . . . yes, ma'am, that is an honor," he said, slowly regaining his composure. "And I'll get you through the rest of this trip, too. You can bet your . . . bottom dollar on it, ma'am."

"Meg," Ma said with a smile. "You must call me Meg."

"Yes, ma'am . . . I mean, Meg." He fumbled with his hat. "I'd better git going. I've got some things to do yet.'' He took a step toward the rear of the wagon, then stopped and turned. ''By the way, Merry Christmas.''

''Christmas?'' I said in disbelief.

''Yup. I checked the calendar this morning.''

''Well, I'll be damned,'' I said.

Nathan glanced my way. ''Most of us are.''

''I don't know about that,'' Doniphan said. He first looked at Nathan, then at Ma. ''You know, I don't suspicion the Lord takes a good view of fighting on Christmas Day, but something tells me He was working our territory today. It surely does.''

Then he tipped his hat to the ladies and left.

It wasn't long before everyone was making excuses to leave, having something or other they had to do, but we all knew it was to give Ma the rest she so well deserved. But it was James's hand she held on to as the boy prepared to go. I was fishing around in Farnsworth's trunk of books looking for one I thought might be appropriate for the day, it being Christmas and all. When I saw Ma tell her grandson to take a seat, I got up figuring they were wanting to be alone.

''No, that's all right, Finn,'' she said. ''What I have to say is nothing to be ashamed of or hidden.''

So I went back to looking through those books, only half listening to Ma and James.

''It's hard, isn't it?'' she said, still holding his hand.

''Huh?'' the boy said, coming out of a daydream he must have had.

''Growing up,'' she said. ''Shooting that man this afternoon.''

''It's nothing like it's supposed to be,'' James said, suddenly speaking as though a flood gate had opened inside him. ''It ain't nothing like the books Finn reads and the stories Grandpa told. It ain't fun at all.''

''I know,'' she said, pausing. ''I wonder sometimes if heroes and heroics shouldn't be left to young boys, old men and story books.''

''But I'm still a boy.''

''Oh, no, James,'' she said as I glanced in her direction, saw her shaking her head as I became more interested in the conversation than my book search. ''You may have a few years to fill out yet, but after what happened this afternoon, you're no longer a boy. You've been through a painful experience, and sometimes those are the most valuable, as hard as they may be.

"You see, we each of us go through life doing what we must, and more often than not, there is no one to cheer us on when we do something worthwhile. And sometimes that will be confusing, for only you will ever know about those heroic deeds you think you have performed." She paused again, as if she were not sure the ten-year-old boy could digest what she spoke of.

"Did Grandpa really name Pa after that hero Nathan Hale?"

"Yes, indeed," she replied, a proudness in her voice. "I might add that your father also has some of that man's qualities."

"I wish I was named after someone famous," the boy said dejectedly.

Ma looked at James in what could only be described as astonishment.

"But you are, child," she said. "You mean you didn't know?"

"Know what?"

"James, there were only two men that your father ever thought to be truly brave and honorable men. One was your grandfather. The other was a man your father claims taught him everything he knows about this wild land you claim. I believe his name was James Bowie."

I could see James's spirits soar for the moment and remembered all those stories Nathan had told us about Bowie and their years together. To hear Nathan talk he was quite a man, that one, with no one to equal him— except maybe Pa. But the smile was short-lived, and I knew the memory of today's events had crawled back inside James as he stared at the floor.

"James," Ma said, and now her voice was soft, filled with the same kind of compassion she had had for us boys as youngsters. "Look at me." When the boy didn't move, she placed a hand on the side of his chin, turning his head slowly to face her. "Listen to me, James," she said, her voice now stern, "and don't ever forget what I tell you now.

"I've never killed a man, and it's not something I believe I'd take pride in. But you're not to be ashamed of what you did this afternoon." Her hand fell to his and she held it tightly, desperately. "What you did is no more than what Mr. Doniphan, Mr. Bowie, or Finn or your father or, especially, your grandfather would have done. And he'd be so proud of you, Liam would." But the expression on James's face didn't change, and for a moment I figured she was thinking the same as me, that she had failed to inspire anything in the boy's mind. Then all of the toughness that had brought her this far suddenly subsided, and all I could see was a woman who could only speak or feel the emotions of a woman in love. A tear ran down her cheek as she said, "You're my only grandson, James, and I could never love you more than I do right now. Don't you see, child? You saved your mother and Lisa and me." Then she gave a long, silent look at the bundle tucked into the covers next to her. "And you gave life." I saw tears in her eyes as she looked back at her grandson. "For if you'd not been here this afternoon, James, I'd not have had this son."

The boy didn't look like he knew what he was supposed to do, but he did the right thing. He and Ma held each other in pure silence for a bit. I found the book I was looking for then and left with James.

"You know, son," I said, closing the flap of the entrance, "if that woman ever had a reason to love you, it was for what you did today."

"How's that?"

"I reckon you got a lot of your grandpa in you." Still, the boy seemed touched with gloom. "Look, James," I said in one last, desperate attempt to make him see the importance of what he had done, "do you remember that marker your pa and me put on your grandpa's grave."

"Yes," he nodded. " 'Born Irish . . . lived, fought and died an American.' Why?"

"Well, James, I've never been sure of too awful much in my life, but after today there is one thing I know for a certainty."

"What's that?"

"When your time comes, they'll be putting the same thing on your tombstone."

"But why?"

I gave him a manly slap on the back.

"Son, you're a Callahan. There ain't no way you could be anything else."

I never will know if it was the slap on the back that did it or not, but a proud smile came to his face then, and I knew one thing for sure: What his grandma had told him and what I had just said were two things that James Callahan would remember for the rest of his life.

Lisa was at the fire, heating up some water while Nathan was fixing up a meal for us when I joined them. The girl seemed just as excited as Ma about the birth of our new brother. When I asked her about it, she smiled briefly, remembering something from the past.

"I suppose that in a way it's sort of funny," she said, still smiling. "You see, that was the reason I was sent to the New York Women's Penitentiary. That was why I stowed away."

"Penitentiary?!" Nathan and I seemed to say it as one.

"Yeah." She had come a long way from being shy since I had first seen her get off that stagecoach. I'll say that for her. "I read the books that were available, and . . ."

"And?"

"And I was serving as a doctor and a midwife both. I was helping women give birth to their children."

"A woman doctor?" Nathan said incredulously.

"I wasn't charging the prices of the local doctors." She shrugged. "I guess it was a matter of politics that I was sentenced to jail. But I did pretty good today, don't you think?"

"Well, sure," I mumbled. "I reckon. Is that why Kragg came after you?"

"That was his excuse," she said. "He had a reputation for being an evil man back in New York who would hire out to the devil or anyone else for the right price. I guess they wanted me back bad enough to have him sent after me."

"Ain't nobody gonna miss him, the way I figure it," Nathan said and went back to cooking our meal as Lisa walked off with her heated water.

* * *

"He had no further intercourse with Spirits, but lived upon the Total Abstinence Principle ever afterward; and it was always said of him, that he knew how to keep Christmas well, if any man alive possessed the knowledge. May that be truly said of us! And so, Tiny Tim observed, God Bless Us, Every One!"

It was nearing midnight when I closed the cover on the Dickens book. The fire was dying down and James was the only one left, propped against my shoulder, asleep. The others had listened to me reading *A Christmas Carol* for as long as they could, then had retired for the night. When James had fallen asleep, I had read the rest of the book to myself, feeling a sense of warmth as I did. We weren't near anything close to what you'd call a home, but maybe it's the celebrating of a day like the birth of Christ that brings out the closeness in men.

It had been quite a day. We had survived a battle against four-to-one odds, saved, most likely, by the fact that the enemy soldiers were firing far too high to do any damage to us. Ma had given birth and I now had a new brother, and my nephew had saved the day by fending off an intruder. And I had stumbled on this Dickens book and liked it.

The sky was clear as I took in the stars. Maybe Doniphan was right. Maybe the Lord was working our territory that day. Slowly, I picked up James, looking down into the innocence in the boy's face as I carried him to the wagon.

"And God Bless Us, Every One," I said.

Chapter 18

After the Battle of El Brazito, Doniphan and his men settled in at El Paso del Norte while they waited for the arrival of an artillery battery they had requested from Santa Fe. The traders set up shop and did a thriving business while they waited. It seemed that all of Doniphan's men were content to wait and rest in this valley that even in this time of year was well stocked with dried fruit and vegetables. Me, I was restless, as was Nathan. Or maybe that's just a family trait.

Ma was doing well with the newborn, and that was fine. But Nathan and me, well, I reckon we were just used to doing something. Around the ranch there had always been things that needed doing, and going from can-see to can't-see was what made the days go by as swiftly as they did.

Doniphan had become friendly with the village *alcalde*, and in desperation we sought him out. If he needed volunteers, Nate and I were the first ones there, and it didn't matter whether it was scouting to the south for enemy soldiers or to the west, chasing the Apaches that often threatened to invade the village.

It was during the first week of February that the courier rode into camp. The two of us had just returned from another scouting party and were tending to our horses when the man came in.

"Either one of you go by the name of Callahan?" He was a gaunt-looking man with a face that was both creased and burned by wind and sun, even in the winter season. Always the suspicious one, Nathan cocked an eye toward the man as he took in his features.

"Well, now, I didn't know they was counting heads this year. Why do you ask?"

"You're a Callahan," the man said, answering his own question.

"How so?"

"He said the big one was a smart-ass what carried a bowie knife, and the skinny one was quiet and had him a book nearby." He glanced at one of my leather-bound books on top of a nearby corral post and nodded in the affirmative. "You're them." Nathan started to grow a right mean look, but the man held up a hand in defense. "Whoa, hoss. I'm just quoting Sam."

"Sam?" There ain't much that Nathan and me ever did together all at one time, except for shooting that fella Kragg, but we both got out the same word at the same time. The man could only be talking of Sam Colt or Sam Walker, and it being so long since we'd heard from either of them, it took us by surprise, I reckon.

"Sam Colt. He paid me fifty dollars to bring these out here to you," he said, pointing to the saddlebags on the horse, "and said he'd give me another fifty if'n I got back with word of your family. You know him, do you?"

"Friends from way back," I said with a smile.

"Well, here they are," the man said, untying the saddlebags and pulling out a thick mahogany case from each of the bags. He handed one to each of us and then fished around in his pocket, finally producing two keys.

Each case contained one of the new Colts, a powder flask, bullet mold, caps and a handful of lead balls, half of them the round type, the others being some newfangled things I had never seen before.

"Well, I'll be damned," Nathan said, a look of amazement crossing his face as he stared at the pistol.

"I'll say" was all I could come up with, for I was as awed as he was.

The rider ate a noon meal with us, filling us in on everything Sam Colt had been up to, including the merger with Whitney in order to get the first orders out.

Apparently, the trip that Sam Walker had mentioned before I left Palo Alto hadn't just been brag, at least if the weapon I was looking at was the end result of it. To call it a Goliath would be putting it mildly. It was 15½ inches long and weighed nearly five pounds. The barrel itself was nine inches long, and the six-shot cylinder was bored for a .44-caliber round, as Sam had spoken of. It had a hinged-lever ramrod for easy seating and reloading of powder and ball. The squareback brass trigger guard and improved shape of the handle, both suggestions of Sam Walker's, looked and felt as if they would greatly improve the handling of the weapon. The cylinder had a fancy scene engraved on it of an Indian fight, likely something Walker had told Colt about. To hear the courier talk, Walker and Colt had worked on the design during the fall, and the official contract had been signed in early January, but Colt had started production of the model before then; he was that confident of what he would call the Walker Colt, in honor of Sam Walker.

According to this fella, Colt was figuring to have the entire order done by summer and into the hands of the military fighting the war by fall. It seemed like an incredible feat, but then, you never could tell about Sam Colt and his tinkering with machines and such. He just might do it. When I asked the man if there was any news of Sam Walker, he frowned as though to dig into his memory. I laced his coffee with a liberal dollop of Taos Lightning, and his memory got better real quick.

"Seems I heard Colt was wanting to keep him there until the guns was finished, but the Army put Walker on orders, and he's supposed to be heading out this way again sometime next month."

"It'll be good to see him again."

Afterward, Mayberry, as he identified himself, was showing us the particulars of the new pistols when Tom Dobie stormed into camp and didn't stop until he came face to face with me. From the look of total frustration and hate on his face, I was near certain he'd start swinging any second.

"I've had it, Callahan! That pilgrim's fired," he said forcefully, pointing a finger at me for emphasis. "I don't care what kind of a deal you made with him. I don't want to see him near those teams again. Understand?"

"Who're you talking about? Farnsworth?"

"Damn right!" he said, then paused, trying to calm down. "Look, the last month or so that man's been about as useful to me as buffalo chips in one of them fancy chef's salads. I don't know what it is, but he ain't talking about it, and he ain't doing, neither.''

"He's awful new out here, Tom," I said. "Why don't you give him another chance?"

"Sonny," he said, glaring down at me. "I've been doing the jobs of three men on this trip, and I damn sure ain't picking up after a fourth. No, I'll work it myself before I take him back."

" 'Scuse me, friend." Mayberry, the courier, stood up, hat in hand. "You're needing someone to work stock, are you?"

"Yeah. You got any experience?"

"Worked for my uncle's freighting outfit for a couple of years back East."

"You're hired," Dobie said, nodding toward the man. "Come with me."

There weren't any scouting parties heading out that afternoon, so when Nathan and I finished loading our mammoth new Colts, we sought out Farnsworth. We found him at the edge of camp, standing alone and staring off into the distance.

"Anything worth looking at out there?" I asked.

"No," the drummer said. "I just . . . wish I was back East. I never should have come in the first place."

"Why?" Nathan asked. "You got my son out of a tight spot twice, saved his life one of those times. Ask me, Farnsworth, that takes guts."

"Yes, but there's nothing but badmen and killing out here! It all seems so futile!"

"Well, hoss, I reckon we got a different view of things out here. Back East, you people take any man who's on the wrong side of the law to be a badman, but out here it's different."

"But how could it be?" he asked. "There has to be law!"

"Couldn't agree with you more," I said. "Trouble is, they ain't too many people come out here ever packed a lawbook along as one of their necessities." I put a hand on the Walker Paterson still on my left hip. "Long as you've got something on the lines of this, you wind up making most of your own law most times.

"As for badmen, I can't say we ever got in the habit of dressing real spiffified like you folks, but don't figure that every man in buckskins with a week's growth of beard is an outlaw. Now, Doniphan and Dobie, you might call them badmen, but I'd never say it thinking they were outlaws. You see, out here a horse thief and a killer is just that. I'd have to say that Tom Dobie is about as honest a man as I run across in some time. But he's a bad man to tangle with, and I'd think twice about getting on his wrong side."

"But the killing," Farnsworth said, a look of anguish on his face. "There's so much of it."

"It ain't like this all the time," Nathan said. "It's just that someone started a war out here and we're stuck in the middle of it. Maybe back East you've got constables and a regular army to protect you, but out here a man has to fend for himself, and I'll tell you right off that anyone threatens me or mine is gonna have to deal with the business end of whatever hardware I'm carrying at the time." He stopped a moment, looked at the smaller man, and it was then I thought I saw a spark of recognition in Nathan's eye. "That's it, isn't it? The reason Dobie says you ain't working right?"

"What?"

"You never killed a man before, did you? Before you shot that one going after James?"

"No," Farnsworth said timidly, speaking almost in a whisper. "It was so horrible, and I don't know why I did it."

"Maybe because you thought James was worth saving."

"No! No! It's not that!" he yelled in the loudest voice I had ever heard him speak in. "I don't want to kill anyone! Don't you understand?"

"You mean you wouldn't even shoot one of them Mexicans if he was coming at you and you knew he was gonna kill you?" I could sense the anger growing in my brother.

"I—I don't know," the little man said, not able to meet Nathan's stare.

"Then maybe I was wrong, Farnsworth," Nathan said. "Dobie said he had no use for a man he had to pick up after, and I damn sure don't have any need for someone who figures everyone else is gonna wet-nurse him 'cause he don't want to do for himself. We get out of this mess,

I'll get you your one-way ticket back to all that safety you enjoy in the East.''

Nathan had become more harsh with the man as he went on, and by the time he finished, there was little doubt as to how he felt about Farnsworth. When he left without a word, the drummer turned to me as though looking for a way out, but I didn't have one.

"He's right, Farnsworth. This is a land of survivors, and if you aren't strong when you come out here, you'd better learn to be real fast if you want to live long.'' I put a hand on his shoulder, trying in some way to show the man I understood. "Maybe it's for the best,'' I said. "Maybe you do belong back East.''

I found Nathan out in the valley, about half a mile from camp. He was picking up thicknesses of wood and placing them atop an old stump. I knew there was nothing I could do to change my brother's mind, not when he got set in his ways like he did, so I put the subject out of my mind and concentrated on what I thought he had come out here for, to test-fire the new Colt.

Over the years we had become used to the kick of the Paterson .41, and it was a good, solid kick that required strong wrists. But something told me that this big gun my brother was now about to fire would need more than your average strong wrist. And I was right, for when Nathan fired it, holding it in only one hand, there was a thunderous echo throughout the valley as his whole arm flew up and backward, nearly over his shoulder.

"Judas Priest!'' I yelled, not sure if anyone could have heard it anyway, for my ears were ringing something fierce. While I waited for my ears to clear, Nathan just stood there, staring at the pistol, a dumbfounded look on his face.

"What the hell was that?'' I faintly heard Tom Dobie ask.

"This.'' Nathan held up the monstrous pistol in his hand.

"Sounds like Sam outdid himself,'' I said.

"Well, you fellas'd better let 'em know you're out here, then,'' Dobie said. "You've got half the camp running around looking for those four-pounders the Mexicans carry.''

"Horse apples!" Nathan said in disgust. "This is gonna be a good gun . . . if I can ever hit anything with it."

"Nathan," I said, "I think you've found that bigger gun you're looking for. Here, let me give her a try." I took the pistol from him and paced off a few yards more to the rear so that I was closer to sixty feet from the target. "Stand back, fellas," I said and then took aim, this time holding the weapon in both hands. When I fired, the same thunderous boom bounced off the walls of the valley.

"Damn, boy," Dobie said. "That's worse than my scattergun."

But I paid little attention to him as I headed for the target to see what I had hit. It took a while to dig it out, but by measure it went a hell of a ways in, and I gave a long, low whistle.

"It cleared a good seven inches of hardwood, fellas, and then some," I said when they arrived. "I'll guarantee you one thing," I added, still somewhat amazed at what I'd just experienced. "The pilgrim that gets hit with this thing ain't going nowhere but down."

We were on the way back to camp when James came running up to us. The boy was clearly excited about something.

"It's Mr. Doniphan! He left word!" the boy said breathlessly. "We're leaving tomorrow!"

Chapter 19

"Answer me something, Doniphan. Just answer me something."

It was Tom Dobie who rode up beside the Missouri commander as I was returning from a scouting mission. We were on our fifth day out of El Paso del Norte and well into another of the many desert crossings that had taken up so much of the journey south of the Rio Grande.

"Yeah, Dobie, what do you want?" From the tone of his voice, I had the idea that Doniphan wasn't any more comfortable with the sudden change of weather than any of the rest of us. It had gone from freezing cold back to the unbearable heat that most deserts get their reputation from. And, true to the stories one tends to hear, it can put a man on edge.

"According to what we heard back in El Paso, General Taylor's got his ass kicked all over the place and is likely prisoner in some Sonora hoosegow."

"Yeah."

"And they were saying that everyone in southern California was getting ready to revolt against us."

"So?"

"And on top of that," Dobie concluded, his own sense of frustration showing, "you get direct word that General Wool has pulled out and left Chihuahua and we're still marching down there. Now, what I want to know is have you gone plum loco or is it you just don't give a damn no more? Which?"

"Hell, man," Doniphan replied. "Someone's got to do it."

When Dobie shook his head in resignation and went

back to tending his stock, I gave thought to what he had said and realized that Doniphan was right. There was little doubt that the way we were going was a hell of a roundabout way to get back to our home, but it also seemed fruitless to have traveled over a thousand miles and fought one minor battle all for nothing. And the longer I knew this Doniphan, the more I was convinced that he intended to give his men what they had signed up for, or at least a good taste of what it might have been like. It seemed unlikely that all of the Mexicans in Chihuahua could have been recruited to overwhelm the Americans. Besides, one thing I had found out since I began fighting Mexicans some ten years back was that they oftentimes got all fired up believing that the *norteamericanos* would cut and run in battle, which was why they seemed so full of fight at the outset. But that false courage had been broken when our lethal firepower cut down their charging infantrymen and volunteers. And when they found out just what they were up against, well, they got a whole lot more thoughtful about the war process. That was why I didn't put much faith in the rumor about Zach Taylor and his army, for the man had fought Indians and Mexicans successfully in the past and was too good a general to lose his command to anyone.

If we had a problem it was going to be getting there, for we had some 250 miles to cover before reaching Chihuahua, a goodly portion of it desert. Doniphan had received his battery of artillery just prior to leaving El Paso, and those men accompanying it brought his field strength to 924. He had also cracked down on the traders and made them form a battalion of their own for defense if and when any fighting started.

It took us three weeks to do it, but somewhere around the end of February we camped about fifteen miles from a creek called the Sacramento, a creek that was again that distance from Chihuahua.

"You're gonna get your fight, Colonel," I said, riding into camp that afternoon as Doniphan and his men settled in. "Those troops in Chihuahua you've been hearing about aren't rumor anymore. I seen 'em with my own eyes, and there ain't no two thousand, like at Brazito." Before he had a chance to say what I figured he would, that he was expecting a smaller force, I let him in on the bad news. "It's more like three thousand regulars and another thousand farmers they've put on a volunteer status, mostly carrying machetes."

"Where did you spot 'em?" Doniphan said, not losing a bit of composure.

"Down the Sacramento. Looks like they're waiting there for us."

"Then we'll take 'em tomorrow," Doniphan said. There wasn't the excitement in his voice that many of his men would give forth, but rather a cold, matter-of-fact assurance. The man simply knew what he had to do and was making ready for it.

We spent a peaceful night, resting for the battle we knew would come tomorrow. I had come to the conclusion that what Lisa Harris had said to my brother was having quite an effect on him. Ever since Brazito, Nathan had taken more of an interest in Ellie, and I found myself scouting without him more and more. But I knew he would pull his share of duty when the time came, so I didn't worry. That night again I saw them head toward the outskirts of the camp, Nathan carrying that huge bearskin Doniphan had given Ma, Ellie sporting the look of a woman who has set her cap for a man. Me and James spent the night reading.

I was checking my loads in the massive Walker Colt the following morning when I heard Tom Dobie talking to Lisa around the corner of their wagon.

"Please be careful, Tom," I heard her say, a note of concern in her voice.

There was a moment of silence before Dobie said, "I'll be back," followed by another pause and, "One thing, Lisa."

It was the softest I'd ever heard Dobie speak. Not that I'm an eavesdropper, you understand.

"Yes, Tom."

"In case I don't make it—"

"No, Tom," she said, and I had a feeling she was holding him tight, for his words were muffled some, as though she were talking to his chest. "No. Don't talk about it. I don't want to hear about it."

There was more silence before Dobie said, "I just wanted to say that . . . well, you asked me one time if I ever loved someone the way Meg loved Liam. I been giving it some thought, Lisa, and I still don't know as I ever did love anyone that way. But . . . if and when this whole mess is over, I'd like to do that with you, if you've a mind to.''

"Oh, Tom," I heard her say, her voice sounding like a mixture of happy crying a woman does and relief. "You don't know how much I've wanted to hear you say that. You really don't know."

"Well, you got your wish," I said, stepping around the corner. Dobie was the more surprised of the two. "That is, if we make it through this day." I could see Dobie wanted to go, but Lisa held on to him tight. "You ready to go, Tom?"

"Yeah, just give me a minute and I'll be right there."

I was fitting the Walker Colt into a makeshift holster I had fashioned for my mount when Dobie joined me.

"You really gonna settle down?"

"I'm gonna try. Won't know unless I try. Just do me a favor, will you?"

"Sure. What is it?"

"In case something happens this time out, in case I don't make it back, take care of her, will you? She's done good by your Ma, so she should deserve at least that in return."

"Don't worry about her, Tom. Ma never turned away someone she knew was in need. Besides, Lisa's almost part of the family now, so she'd likely be stuck with us anyhow. You just concern yourself with getting through this day. Being outnumbered four-to-one ain't my favorite fighting odds, and we're gonna need every man we've got.''

"Except Farnsworth." He pondered his own statement a moment. "You didn't *really* leave him behind to protect the women, did you? Hell, they've got a better chance of surviving with James there alone than for what Farnsworth's worth."

"I found out why he hasn't been worth a damn since El Brazito."

"Oh?" Dobie asked with more than a casual interest.

"I reckon some people never get used to killing, and Farnsworth is one of 'em. So let's just say I want to keep him safe and sound until we can ship him back

East, where he belongs. At least if he can't protect the women in the wagon, James can protect him." I chuckled to myself. "According to Nathan, though, the little bastard would turn over all of my gold if anyone came running at him hard. Says he figures he's that kind."

"For your sake, Callahan, I hope you're wrong."

"We'll see," I said and spurred my horse on.

Doing the unorthodox was getting to be a way of life for Doniphan and his men, for that was exactly what we did that morning breaking camp. The trail we were on would lead us into an ambush that would likely wipe out most of our force. So when I saw what Doniphan had his men doing, I figured I knew what he was up to. Sort of.

Doniphan formed his wagons into four columns, running them parallel to one another, as though he were readying for an Indian attack on the Santa Fe Trail. If a body could divide this ragtag outfit into infantry, cavalry and artillery, you could say he placed those units in between the columns where they would be ready for use when called upon. Oh, we followed that trail all right, just like that, until we neared the Sacramento. Then the Missourian gave his outfit a flanking movement and we proceeded to cross an arroyo. That didn't seem no trouble, but by the time we reached safety, the frustrated enemy had spotted us and opened fire on us at a distance that was well out of range.

When Doniphan saw the panoplied lancers forming for a charge, he ordered his artillery to open fire. The rest of us, both a-horse and afoot, sat by and watched as the withering fire shattered the attackers. We sat there for near an hour while those cannons went off one after the other, and I do believe I hadn't seen a group of men so anxious to get into battle and being held back by so strong a commander since Sam Houston and his boys took San Jacinto. Finally, to take up time, some of the men began placing bets on where the next shell would land, and I found myself thinking of Lisa's comment about how men treated the war as a game. Most of these men were far from their youth, but to watch them place a bet, not knowing if they'd live out the day to collect it, well, they sure did look like they were enjoying their youth again.

When the Mexicans made another charge, it was toward the rear and the wagons. Without a word, we knew what was happening, and Dobie and I swung our mounts around, heading toward our wagon. It seemed like we had only taken a few strides with our mounts when Nathan pulled up beside us out of nowhere. None of us spoke, for it was a time for doing, not palavering.

We charged straight into them right off. A dozen of the Mexican soldiers were converging on the wagon, but we were still too far off to throw any effective firepower at them. As they neared the camp I could see the desperation in Nathan's and Dobie's eyes, the kind of look that says they'd sell their soul to the devil or fight him on his own terms if only they could save the ones they loved. Then, just when it looked hopeless, just when they had come upon the wagon, the damndest thing happened!

Of a sudden Farnsworth appeared from the side of the wagon. He had one of my Colt revolvers and, holding it in both hands, began firing at whoever got nearest to him. Nathan and Dobie must have been as amazed as I was, for there were five bodies falling every which way, and it passed through my mind that the little fella had bottom after all. By God, he'd do, he would. It was thinking that that got us there faster, or maybe seeing what the drummer was doing is what did it. I don't know. All I know is there were five enemy bodies on the ground and Farnsworth lying there propped up against a wheel, bloodied up his own self.

But there were still more coming, and we rode into them like a blue norther, hard, quick and angry. I heard Tom Dobie's shotgun go off twice and thought I saw him disappear from his horse. Nathan and me barreled over whatever we didn't hit, staying on our horses till we were in about the middle of the bunch. I felt something hot on my side and used my last bullet killing the pilgrim carrying the lance. Nathan was gone from his horse now, and I got to figuring that being the only one atop a horse made me a hell of a target, so I jumped off, too. I took my knife to one and didn't notice much movement around me after that. Looking around, I saw Nathan swinging an enemy rifle at several unarmed soldiers while Tom Dobie was doing the same with his shotgun and a half-dozen traders shot away the rear end of what was left of the marauders.

The traders had done a fine job of beating back the enemy from their own wagons, and when the gunfire in our area died down, the camp seemed deathly quiet.

Lisa and James jumped from the back of the wagon, Lisa spotting Dobie while James stood in awe of the number of dead men in the area. I think we all of us saw Farnsworth at the same time, propped up against the wheel, his shirtfront all covered with blood.

"You all right, hoss?" Nathan said, although we all knew the man was dying.

"I saved it!" the little drummer said, a wild look in his eye as he placed a bloody hand on Nathan's wrist. "I saved the gold!"

"That don't matter, hoss," I heard Nathan say. "You saved the women, and that's what's important. I reckon I was wrong about you."

"I never wanted to kill anyone," Farnsworth said. "It just . . . it just . . ."

"You done fine, Farnsworth," I said. "Just fine." But I was talking to a dead man.

Tom Dobie looked to be about half-dead as Lisa supported him, bringing him into camp from the far side. He was minus a shirt-sleeve that looked to be bound to his shoulder to stem the flow of blood. He wasn't more than half-conscious, so I picked him up and carried him back to the wagon, Nathan helping me get him inside. Once we had him inside, I got up to leave, but Lisa grabbed my arm.

"Hey, mister, you got a cut side," she said. "Did you know that?"

I glanced down at my side, all of a sudden aware of the lancer who had tried to kill me earlier. My side was bloodstained, the warmth becoming more evident as I stared at it.

"Sit down," Lisa said in a commanding voice. "It won't take but a minute to fix. Besides, this war ain't going no place."

I seemed to be drawing an audience, so I started giving out commands of my own, just to be doing something.

"Nathan, get this thing reloaded," I said, tossing the

Paterson to him. Ma and Ellie said they were fine and Tom Dobie was coming to. "You still got a good hand," I said when he looked at me. "Think you can make sure these women stay alive if those Mexicans give this another try?"

"Bank on it," he said, and I knew from the conviction in his voice that wounded or not, he meant it. "Just load up my shotgun and set by a couple of those pistols of yours, and me and James'll make 'em think twice before they come a-knocking again. Right, son?"

"You bet, Tom," the boy said with enthusiasm. I had a feeling he figured he was a full-fledged fighting man now, and although he may have lacked size, he likely was.

"Good," I said as Lisa finished tying the bandage at my side. "Nathan and me are gonna check back with Doniphan. They're still shooting out there, so you can bet this fracas ain't through yet."

When we got back to Doniphan, the man was cussing a blue streak, and it was hard to tell if he was happy or mad. The First Missouri had worked to within four hundred yards of the parapets from which the Mexicans were firing without even taking aim; they were that scared.

"Look at them boys!" he yelled as we watched two companies swarm the parapets, fighting with pistols, knives, rifles, muskets, fists and anything else they could get their hands on. "By God, they ain't afraid of nothing!"

I was checking my loads, about to start forward into the foray, when I felt the strong hand of Doniphan on my arm. He was silent now, and I followed his glance to the right flank, where a number of the enemy were trying to escape.

"Why don't you boys get a couple of mine and see can you stop 'em."

"Right."

With a dozen others, we chased the enemy most of the rest of that afternoon. On more than one occasion, we spotted some soldiers who had the good fortune to find horses and were in the process of escaping. And each time, either Nathan or me dismounted, stood stock-still, took dead aim on the rider and shot him out of the saddle with that newfound cannon we each had. And

ach time we did, it thoroughly amazed the riders with
us.

When we got back it was near nightfall, and the sur-
geons were doing their best to patch up those needing it
most. The battleground was silent and the Mexicans
were in full retreat, a number of them, I found out,
having been killed while trying to escape to the mountains,
where they had been done in by Apaches who had taken
a ringside seat to watch us finish one another off.

But only one of Doniphan's men, a sergeant, had been
killed. The only other American killed had been a trader.
And Farnsworth. Other than that there were only seven
wounded in Doniphan's force in what his men were
calling the Battle of Sacramento. Doniphan had taken
forty Mexicans prisoner, killed three hundred and
wounded an equal number, it was said. And, once again,
he and his men had broken the resistance in the area.

Two days later, Doniphan and his men occupied
Chihuahua.

We buried Farnsworth the next morning. Nathan and
James did the digging, since they were the only ones
who hadn't been wounded all that serious in the battle.
But I watched Nathan doing it and knew, somehow, that
digging that grave was as painful for him as any wound
he had ever suffered. No one knew his date of birth, so
the cross simply read "Oliver T. Farnsworth, died 28
February, 1847." Nailed on to the bottom of the cross
was another grotesquely shaped piece of wood. But it
was the only wood Nathan could find, and when I saw
what he had penned into it as the drummer's epitaph, I
knew how bad my brother felt about Farnsworth's dying.
In bold letters, it read

"HE DIED RIGHT . . . GIVING HIS LIFE FOR HIS FRIENDS."

Chapter 20

I'll tell you, hoss, no one ever looked less like heroe than Doniphan and his men. If the cut of their cloth wa a bit below average when they left Fort Leavenworth well, I can guarantee it was getting down to nothing on a good many of them! Fact is, when we rode into Chihuahua the American residents who rushed out to greet us with a hero's welcome rushed right back inside their home when they saw us. Someone said they even locked thei doors first, figuring us for Apaches!

But I was one of the first to arrive in town, and afte they got over the shock of seeing us, I was able to ge directions to a decent doctor, who agreed to come out to the edge of town and take a looksee at Tom Dobie' wounds. The doctor, a middle-aged Mexican, gave hin the once-over and said that although he had lost blood his wound would heal properly with rest. I dug into my pocket and pulled out another of those gold pieces a payment to the doctor. It sure was strange how awestruck people were getting when they saw those pieces of gold

"You sure do get awful free with that stuff," Dobi said.

"Don't worry," I said confidently. "There's mor where that came from."

"I hope you're right, friend. It's just that I got th feeling this dream of yours ain't gonna pan out."

With that I pulled out Farnsworth's trunk and un packed all of the books until I could remove the fals bottom of the trunk. I counted out the gold, settin Farnsworth's small amount to one side.

"Close to a thousand that I can figure," I said as Dobi

ave a low whistle of admiration. "That ought to be nough to get anyone started out in this country, if you sk me."

"I won't argue that," Tom said. "And if that's the ase, then it's just a matter of picking a spot. You boys ive much thought to that, yet?"

"No, can't say as I have." To be truthful, I hadn't nought about it since St. Louis when we had made the riginal decision to come west with Doniphan's outfit. Jor had Nathan spoken of it that I knew. "I reckon we een spending most of our time on trying to stay alive le last few months more than giving any serious thought) where we'd wind up."

I brought the subject up at supper that night, but little as settled about what our final destination would be.

"Boys," Ma said, "as long as I have someplace to all a home and raise your little brother, it won't matter at ll where it is to me. As long as I know that I've got amily nearby that I can count on if something happens. .ight now that child is the only thing that matters to me a this world."

"And Ma and Lisa will go anywhere you and Tom ay, Pa," James said, suddenly taking on a more grown-up ble. "You know that."

"That leaves you and Finn," Nathan said to his son.

"Don't make a difference to me, Nathan," I said. As long as I've got a place to put this library of mine. hat's all I'm needing." That is, I thought to myself, ntil I find a place I can call a home for Tally.

"What about you, James?"

The boy squinted into the flames of the slowly dying ampfire, then glanced back at Nathan.

"I reckon as long as it's away from those cities, it'll e all right with me," he said.

"Why, James!" Ma said in surprise. "Here I thought ou liked the cities your grandpa and I showed you!"

"Oh, I did, Grandma, but I ain't for sure I'd ever ant to live there. Just seems like a lot of nosy people ll having the need to know what everyone else is doing. a says he don't like cities because of that, and I think e's right."

"Looks like you and me do the picking," Dobie said.

"And all I'm interested in is staying west of the Missis
sippi and out of them cities, like James."

"Well, I'd have to give some more thought to it,"
Nathan said, "but until I do, I figure we can start head
ing back to the U.S. of A." Glancing my way, he added
"What do you say, Finn? How about we get resupplie
tomorrow and get a move on and see if the rest of tha
treasure of yours is still waiting for you?"

"Suits me."

The next day we took an inventory of what we woul
need and enlisted James and Nathan to do the errand
involved in obtaining the goods. It was on one of the
return trips that Nathan had a grin like the cat that at
the fish.

"You ain't gonna guess what Doniphan just told me."

"What's that?"

His grin broadened. "He just got word that Taylor'
army won a big battle at a place called Buena Vista
couple of weeks back. But he just barely did it. An
who do you think he was fighting?"

"I never could keep track of those Mexican general
as many of them as there were," I said. "Who?"

"Santa Anna."

"You're joshing me," I said, purely surprised. "Yo
mean that fanatical old reprobate is leading the sheep t
the slaughter again?"

"Yup. And getting himself kicked all over the place
as usual," Nathan said. "And probably claiming victor
back down south.

"Doniphan's saying if we hadn't run into those Mex
cans up here, they would have been down south wit
Santa Anna and have really given Taylor one helluv
beating."

"I doubt it," I said. "Taylor's too good a soldier t
lose to the likes of Santa Anna, even if he'd been figh
ing with these forces here, too."

In two days we had all we thought we would need fo
the trip, including an additional rain barrel attached t
the Conestoga. But I didn't say anything about my ow
plans until after supper that night.

"The way I figure it," I said, "me and James'll rid
ahead and be at Palo Alto when you pull up there."
glanced at Nathan and Tom Dobie. "You two ought t

be able to manage for the women here. And the time it'll take you to get there is what James and I will need to dig up what's left of that gold.''

"Sounds good to me," Tom said. "Maybe by then you'll know where you want to settle, too.''

"Might surprise you," I said with a smile.

The next morning we were readying to leave when Doniphan stopped by. "I'm glad you decided to come with us, Callahan," he said, sticking out a gigantic paw.

"Our pleasure, Colonel," I said, shaking his hand.

"No, Callahan. Ours. You've got some beautiful women in that family of yours. You make sure and take damn good care of them, or I'm gonna come after you," the man chided, "and I won't need none of these yahoos to take care of you," he added, throwing a thumb over his shoulder at his men.

"I do believe you would, Doniphan," I said. "I honest to God do.''

"Luck to you, Callahan," the big man said in parting. "I hope you find what you're looking for.''

"I intend to, Doniphan," I said over my shoulder as we rode out. "I intend to.''

James and I didn't leave the wagon until two days later, when we reached the Conchos River. When we did, I told Nathan and Dobie to follow the Conchos north into the Rio Grande and then cut back south, all the time following the rivers until they came to Palo Alto and Resaca de La Palma, where we would be waiting for them.

"At least you'll have a steady supply of water while you travel," I said. "I don't ever want us to have to go through the spells of drought we had coming down here.''

I could well appreciate the high spirits and enthusiasm of James as we left, for I remembered my own on such adventures when I first came west. And it was that memory that made me choose him over one of the others. The whole past year had been one big series of adventures for him, and there was no reason for him not to have another before returning home.

It took four days of hard riding to reach Palo Alto, but all the time we were on the trail, I had the feeling we were being watched. Somewhere out there, my instincts told me, the Mexicans or Apaches were going to jump us. And I don't mind telling you that the feeling got worse as the days went by. The only thing that kept me going then was the certain knowledge of what I would find when we reached our destination.

It was noon of the fourth day when we reached it, and it hadn't changed, not one bit. The clump of chaparral from which I had shot the soldier was still in its place. The river had flooded at some time or another, but the water level seemed about as it had nearly a year ago when I had stumbled across the poor old man digging the last of the seven holes. We made noon camp and I took James on a tour of the area, showing him the various places I remembered and the events that had taken place what seemed like an eternity ago. When we returned to the area, I ground-tied the horses near the clump of chaparral, out of sight, and brought two shovels to the spot I remembered the hole's being near. After two shovelfuls of sand we struck bone.

"I'd bet money they belong to the old man," I said, and continued to dig. When we were three feet down, I struck metal. This time it was the locker with the gold coins that I'd buried. I busted a lock off with the shovel and opened it up, and sure enough it was at least half-full of gold coins, just like the ones I'd been spreading around for the past year.

"I never did believe in breaking my back when someone could do the work for me."

The voice was strangely familiar, and when I looked up, I saw Ab Sharpson, a gun in his hand aimed right for my belly.

"Ab? I thought you were with the Rangers down with Taylor at Buena Vista."

"Leave of absence," the grizzled old-timer said, a crooked grin on his face. He gave a quick glance at the hole I stood in. "I knew you'd come back for the rest."

"What do you mean? The only other person who knew about this gold was—" I stopped short, realizing too late that Ab knew.

"Excluding you, that would leave the old man that got killed over it," he said, the grin widening.

Then it started coming to me as everything fell into place.

"No wonder Garvey was so shook up when I beat him that day," I said. "He *didn't* know what I was talking about. He *wasn't* lying."

"Yeah," Sharpson chuckled, "you got old Garvey worked up, all right." He still wore the same velvet vest and frock coat I had always seen him in, the stovepipe hat topping his head. "Better toss your gun out and drop that shovel real easy, Finn. You too, son."

We did as he said, climbing out of the hole. When he saw James glance at the Hawken rifle propped against the chaparral, Sharpson slowly shook his head. "That wouldn't be healthful, son. A man could get killed thinking heroics like that, and you ain't even 'tween hay and grass yet."

James stood his ground as Ab Sharpson spit chewing tobacco to the side, wiping the coat sleeve of his free hand across his face. And that was when I knew what it was that had kept jarring at my memory, hidden behind the door that wouldn't open.

"That's what it was," I found myself saying to myself. "It was Garvey's horse I was tracking, but there was something that was phony about it each time that I couldn't pin down."

"And what was that?"

"Garvey didn't chew. Each time I tracked him from the spot of a shooting, I got a description of his horse, but never the rider. And somehow that cud of tobacco next to the hoofprints never seemed right." Now I knew why. I looked at James. "Meet your grandpa's killer." I pushed my hat back and wiped the sweat from my forehead. "James, how about getting us some water? This digging can do a man in."

The boy only glanced briefly from me to Ab, then walked to the horse, whose left side was facing me.

"You stay on this side, son, in my sight, or I'll shoot your friend here on the spot, understand?"

"Yes, sir," James replied, changing course. If the boy was scared, he didn't show it.

"Why'd you do it, Ab? Why try to kill me?"

"I'm a gambler, Finn. You know that. I reckon the story's as old as the hills. Too many debts and not enough money to cover 'em. Can't offer more'n that for an excuse, but it's good enough for me."

"I can't reach it, Finn."

James had a hand stretched nearly halfway over the saddle horn of my horse. I frowned, for the boy had never had any trouble with it before, even from the far side of the saddle.

"You mind if I get it, Ab? You've got my guns, and this heat is drying me out." I was feeling dry in the throat all right, but it wasn't for lack of water.

"Same thing applies, Finn," the man said with a nod of approval. "Stay in sight or the boy gets it. And be slow how you move."

I was getting mad about the whole business. Traveling all this way to find out that the gold I had buried would now be stolen. Then being held at gunpoint by a man I had trusted for some time. And now this boy couldn't reach a canteen of water he'd had no trouble with before. I'll tell you, I was getting mad for a fact. Which accounted for the look of disappointment on my face as I sauntered over to the horse.

"Son, I'm either getting old faster than I ought to be, or you ain't growing as fast as you should," I said, approaching the horse. "Now, what kind of problem have you got here?" I reached a long arm over the saddle horn, but what it landed on sent a quick shiver down my spine. It wasn't the canteen that James had gotten hold of on the far side of my mount. It was the Walker Colt! I had forgotten completely about it! I was so used to carrying the Paterson that I had forgotten all about the Walker!

"Like I said, Finn," James said, "I can't reach it." The boy had seen enough bloodshed in the past year to know what might happen now, but it was clear that the choice was mine to make. One or both of us could die if I made the wrong choice, and it wasn't a choice I wanted to make.

"I see what you mean," I said, bringing the canteen over the saddle horn and handing it to James. All I could do now was trust that he would know what to do, know that he must get out of the line of fire, for I had had my fill of being potshot and threatened. That I had.

"Thanks," the boy said, taking the canteen and shaking it before unscrewing the cap. "Not much left," he added and began to move away from me. When I reached over the saddle a second time, Sharpson immediately motioned me to stop.

"I got another full one, Ab," I said. I could see the man was ready to shoot and froze in my tracks, my hand resting on the Walker Colt.

"Don't be wandering off on me, sonny," Sharpson said. He now had the gun held between the two of us, aimed at no one in particular. James had moved a good twelve feet from my horse now and was taking another step.

"Did you really kill my grandpa, mister?"

"Afraid so, son. It's a hard land. Now, stop moving."

But the boy took one more step away, then another, before he stopped.

"There's something you gotta know, mister. Something you gotta know before you die—" That boy sure had all of his pa in him, for it was something Nathan would say.

I did it in one motion. Swung around to face Ab Sharpson, cocking the Walker as I did. As I did, I felt the thud of a slug smash into my saddle and the horse began to buck. Ab was cocking his pistol for a second shot when I got my other hand on the Walker and squeezed tight and pulled the trigger. A blast of flame and gunpowder smoke erupted then, and I thought I saw the outlaw's body jerk sharply backwards before the black powder engulfed the area.

"You all right, James?" I asked when I heard no other sound from the dying man.

"Sure. How about you?"

I didn't answer, instead walked over to the body of Ab Sharpson. The man had taken the bullet in the chest and now lay in a pool of blood that gushered from his back as well as his chest.

"How could you?" the dying man asked. "We were friends."

"Like the storybooks say, Ab, that was once upon a time," I said. My eyes never left him, but it was to James I now spoke. "James, there's only one thing harder than killing a man you don't know, and that's killing a man you do know. If you're lucky, you'll never know that feeling." I was looking at him hard and mean now and I wanted him to know it before he died. "Killing you was the easiest thing I ever done, Sharpson. Believe me, it was easy.''

The man's head slumped to the side and I saw James, a bit confused, look at the dead man, then at me.

"Was that true what he said, Finn? About being friends?''

"It was true, son. The thing is, James," I said, giving him a serious look, "you don't ever want to put your friends above your kin. Now, if it had been anything else he had done, I might have had second thoughts, but that man killed my Pa, and when you take something like that away from a man . . . well, I reckon revenge comes easy. Besides, like the man said, it's a hard land.''

We buried him in the same hole we had been digging, but I could tell James was a bit squeamish about throwing sand on all of that blood-and-guts body. I found just over a thousand dollars in gold in the old locker. When we got ready to leave the next day, I divided up the gold into our saddlebags and several empty flour sacks I had brought along, and I tied them to the backs of our horses, but the boy just sat atop his mount, looking silently at the unmarked grave.

"It don't seem right, Finn," he said. "No marker, no epitaph."

"Believe me, son," I said with as much conviction as I could, "a man like that's better off forgotten. If he had an epitaph it would only read something like 'He played out a losing hand.' You ask me, he got off fine just being buried. Could have left him to the buzzards, you know.''

We followed the Rio Grande north by west and it was two days later that we met up with Nathan and Dobie out in front of the wagon. The women were full of questions, but the two men seemed content to wait until we set up camp for the night to listen to our story.

"Turns out we got us a right smart amount of gold," I said. "Right, James?"

"Yes, sir.''

"That'd make a small fortune we've got," Tom Dobie said. When I nodded in agreement, he added, "You give any thought to where we could build these women a home?''

"Matter of fact, I did, hoss." I paused a moment to collect my thoughts. "Ellie, didn't Lije spout off quite a bit about those Shining Mountains he thought were so beautiful?''

"He sure did," she said, and I could see she was getting as excited as James had been.

"Well, I don't know about you people, but I've had about enough sand and flatland for one year. I say we turn these horses around tomorrow and head on back through Santa Fe and give those mountains a gander.''

And that is just what we did.

As for the other six holes and what was buried in them, no one ever has found the Lost Treasures of Palo Alto and Resaca de La Palma, but many have tried. Mostly, they find the bones of those who dared to look before them and were foolish enough to continue looking.

Me, I never needed more than I found that day. All the gold in the world couldn't compare to what I'd found in Tally. Someday, sometime, I'd send for her.

About the Author

Jim Miller began his writing career at age ten when his uncle presented him with his first Zane Grey novel. A direct descendent of Leif Erikson and Eric the Red, and a thirteen-year army veteran, Mr. Miller boasts that stories of adventure flow naturally in his blood.

When not busy writing about the future exploits of the Callahan brothers, Mr. Miller spends his time ensconced in his 2,000-volume library filled mostly with history and research texts on the Old West.

The author lives in Aurora, Colorado, with his wife and their two children.